A novel of expl... adventure in the era of sexual permissive ness ... A novel of flesh set on fire ... of lovers blessed with incredibly rich and erotic fantasy lives suddenly realized in a dazzling new world of erotic reality ... A new ecstatic experience for those millions of readers devoted to the bestselling erotic novels by Anonymous.

Also in Arrow by Anonymous

HER

HIM

ME

THEM

YOU

US

I

WOMAN

TWO

BY ANONYMOUS

ARROW BOOKS

Arrow Books Limited
17-21 Conway Street, London, W1P 6JD

An imprint of the Hutchinson Publishing Group

London Melbourne Sydney Auckland
Johannesburg and agencies
throughout the world

First published in Great Britain 1983 by Arrow Books
Published by arrangement with Bantam Books
Reprinted 1983 and 1985

© Bantam Books, Inc.1982

Printed and bound in Great Britain by
Anchor Brendon Limited, Tiptree, Essex.

ISBN 0 09 931680 3

For the Two that is One

Author's Preface

From the Apocryphal New Testament, The Gospel According to the Egyptians in the Second Epistle of Clement:
"When ye have trampled on the garment of shame . . . the two shall be one, the outside as the inside, and the male with the female, neither male nor female."

This novel by Anonymous, *Two*, tells the love story of a man and a woman who, having trampled on the garment of shame, become as one.

There is a curious pattern in the novels Anonymous has given to millions of readers, an underlying unity which can be discovered and appreciated only by rereading each of these novels in the sequence in which they were written and published. It is my most fervent wish that many readers will do just that.

The first, *Her*, is a simple love story between a lonely woman and a lonely man.

Him is the novel of a sexual trinity, two women and one man.

Us is the delineation in human forms—three men and one woman—of the profoundly mysterious saying of the ancient Maria Prophetissa, "Sister of Moses": *One becomes Two, Two becomes Three, and out of the Third comes the One as the Fourth.*

You is an effort on the part of Anonymous to return to the simplicity of a man and a woman in love; but their deep love is contaminated by the others, male and female, who become involved in their sex life during the barren years in which they are apart.

Me, again, is a pair—innocent Candides of the flesh —who do not recognize how mercenary and merciless humans of the several sexes exploit them . . . but who win through to a shared happiness by sheer virtue of that innocence.

Them is one woman plus the world of men, *I* is one man plus the world of women; both encompass the utter complexity of the human equation, in which the woman (in *Them*) explores the universe of the flesh through sex, as the man (in *I*) explores through sex the universe of the spirit.

In *Two*, as in the beginning with *Her*, Anonymous has returned to the simple, pure love of a Man for a Woman, a Woman for a Man. In this novel, however, each is already a part of a long-established pair that, on the surface, is perfect.

Anonymous, with the progression of characters created in the writing of this series, has arrived at the philosophical and spiritual conclusion that Life and Love call not for Perfection, but for Completeness.

It is *completeness* for which we individual human beings so desperately yearn. Completeness in the flesh as in the soul; so, for both, the only true completion is in the pair, the couple, the You and the I, the Two of us together.

So Anonymous can say again, as Anonymous said in the beginning with the publication of *Her*: "*I have tried to tell . . . a true and simple love story—the truth as real as the simplicity. It seems to me that, in these recent years since the censorship bars have been lowered, the language of love, following Gresham's Law, has been debased into a coarse coinage, with neither tenderness nor love—nor, indeed, any true emotion at all. It has been my ardent desire to new-mint these words, this language, by writing them in the context in which they are most often spoken. For this, the earthy language of love, is the best and truest tongue in the world.*"

Anonymous
The Author of
Her   *Him*
Us   *You*
Me   *Them*
I   &   *Two*

TWO

It can happen by moon or by sun, in rain or in sunshine. It can occur amid extraordinary circumstances, or during the most ordinary of days. It almost never happens when one is looking for it; the very act of seeking, the presence of need, seems to keep it from happening.

However it happens, it comes as a lovely surprise, in a lifting of life, in a surging of blood; and once more the world is a place of beauty, perceived by heightened senses.

However or wherever, for whatever reason or nonreason, it happens to us, once again we have love.

This is how it happened to them.

The Woman:

She would be home soon, ending the dreary milk run to grocery and drugstore and dry cleaner. The house would be gratefully empty, for only yesterday she had delivered over the care, custody, and entertainment of Nancy and Pam, the Gold Dust Twins of her loins, for six blessed weeks of summer camp, and it would be at least two hours before Hale got home from the office. Two hours in which to lie down in a darkened room in a filmy robe; a time, perhaps, when she would slide a questing finger down her flank, to touch . . .

No. It would not occur in that ordinary, expected way. There would, instead, happen to her an Adventure.

Just inside the back door, her arms full of groceries, she hears a knocking at the front. She hurries to put the sacks on the kitchen table and answer the summons.

He is wearing jeans and a checked shirt, blue and white, the short sleeves revealing muscular upper arms. There is a heavy tool belt sagging about his loins. His lean body is lithe and young, younger than hers; so much younger it makes a lump of regret and loss in her throat.

"Yes?"

She likes the cool tone of the inquiry, because it belies the secret, quickening beat of her heart.

He has a nice smile. "Your telephone was reported out of order. I've checked the outside connection, but I need to check inside, too."

"Of course. It's in the kitchen."

She stands aside, but not by much. As he brushes past her, she catches a whiff of male sweat, a sensuous aroma that prickles the downy hair on her arms. For she knows. Already, she knows.

She watches him proceed, all business, into the kitchen. She watches while he dials the secret number they always seem to dial, speaks briefly, hangs up.

2

He turns, shrugging. "Seems to be all right. Somebody must have made a mistake."

She is looking at him, as he is looking at her. But he doesn't know. Not yet.

She feels her breath catch in her throat. "There's another phone in the bedroom. Hadn't you better check that one, too?"

A gallant, daring tone to his voice. "Just show me the way to your bedroom, lady."

So young. The thigh muscles under those tight jeans ripple with the strength of youth. There will be a leanness in the belly, a drive in the legs . . .

Silently she leads the way, feeling it gathering in her, sweetly, at the pit of her stomach. She is acutely aware of him, walking behind her, close enough to touch. She has a sudden apprehension that he is on the verge of doing just that, stroking her ass with his hand, then cupping warmly.

She doesn't want it to happen; she would only have to deny the too-bold gesture with indignation, making a breach in the texture of desire that is weaving itself so sensuously and secretly between them.

Because she doesn't want it to happen, it does not happen. She stands aside as he sits on the edge of the bed to check the instrument. He listens seriously to the dial tone, dials seriously that secret number, speaks monosyllabically, hangs up.

"No trouble on that line, either," he says. He looks at her again, standing before him, and this time he knows. Still sitting, his arms reach to receive her as she comes to him.

She stands trembling as his strong hands clasp her ass, holding her against his face. He breathes deeply, deeply, sniffing her like a male animal testing the air for a female in heat.

"Yes," he says in a husky voice. "Yes, indeed."

She puts her hands on his head, holding it against her body; she yields willingly when he lays her on her back in the bed. He comes over her, his eyes gazing deeply into her eyes, one hand moving surely to the center of her being; not stroking, not yet, simply cupping her nest, making sure of

3

her moist warmth. The tool belt, caught between their bodies, bruises her flesh with the cold rigidities of plier handles and screwdrivers, the massive brass buckle embossing itself on her flesh. It is both a promise and a hurt.

She wants to touch him as intimately as he is touching her. His bird, she knows, will be large and smooth and young under the stroking palm of her hand—and ready, ready, for youth is always ready.

Because it would be an awkward stretch, she does not make the attempt; she simply lies in his arms, his hand now beginning to move on her, stroking and pressing at the same time, making her arch against the pressure.

She hears the catch in his breathing when his palm realizes that only the thinness of a summer dress separates him from the reality of her warm nest. She laughs secretly, remembering how this morning she decided against putting on underpants because today there would be—there must be—an Adventure.

He rises from her, leaving her flesh deprived. But quickly his hands unbuckle the tool-heavy belt sagging so suggestively about his loins. It thuds to the carpet. More slowly, he takes off his shirt, drops it to the floor, zips open the fly, pushes down the denims.

Time for her breath to catch now: he is immediately naked. A darkness to the flesh, smooth as dark marble; Italianate, she decides, the black hair tufted on his chest and, thickly, around his bird, leaving the lean belly smooth and hairless. She watches the muscles in his thighs ripple as he advances upon her.

Reverently he lifts up her dress, folds it back against her stomach. For a long minute he gazes heavy-lidded, half-smiling. She looks while he looks.

His bird is thick, long, the head hidden still because he is uncircumcised. She reaches with two delicate fingers, lifting her shoulders to accomplish it, and pushes back the concealing membrane. The bulbous head shows forth in full glory, a glowing redness of ready; with a moan of anticipation she reaches further still, with both hands, to clasp his buttocks, bring him full upon her.

4

Without the necessity of seeking, his bird finds her nest, strokes deeply into her as she yields backward, lifting her legs to encircle his buttocks, pulling his beautiful dark-fleshed bird into her warm nest . . .

A shout, panicky, angry, and the squealing of brakes as she instinctively brought the heavy station wagon to a shuddering halt. Her senses swam dizzily up out of the depths of sensuous self-preoccupation, leaving her addled with the abrupt dislocation of time and place.

She was driving a strange road she had never taken home from the supermarket. No houses here, only open fields populated by a solitary horse. She turned trembling, afraid to look. Beside the road lay a crumpled bicycle.

The Man:

Thursday afternoon was his time to be alone; he had long since established that fact at home and office. He no longer played tennis, though once he had played tennis well indeed. Not even golf, like so many men of his age and station in life. No games at all that required a forgathering with other human beings.

He had chosen Thursday because, on that day of the week, Eleanor's duplicate-bridge club met. That minimal solitude was the only way to sustain the secret life he lived inside his head. It was a life secret from the bank; the negotiations with clients, the paper work, the meetings of the loan committee—all the many duties and responsibilities that earned him the necessities and luxuries of a placid life. Secret as well from Eleanor, his wife, from the boys, twins of his loins, from the myriad friends and acquaintances of his social circle.

He was, it seemed to him, three separate men inside one husk of human flesh. The Bank Vice-President who, in time, would reach the pinnacle of the presidency because he dutifully kept all fences properly mended. The Husband-and-Father, presiding over a serene household as a Husband-and-Father should, servicing both wife and children with the love, the attention, the income due their status as *his* children, *his* wife.

These two personae, he had realized with the passing of time, had become ever more ghostly presences; though everyone about him seemed to accept without question their reality.

Neither persona was the real *Him*.

Who—he pondered as he laid out the weight-lifting equipment in the empty half of the garage—was the real *Him*? Only this Thursday Man, solitary, dedicated to the physical self? Or did the real *Him* dwell somewhere beyond that cherished image, a stranger to his own feeling and instinct?

He was wearing today pale blue shorts so tight they revealed, rather than concealed, his male secrets. A pale blue T-shirt and a fresh pair of shorts lay ready for the run on the bicycle; for the weight lifting, he kept his top half bare so he could watch the play of muscles as he paced himself through the strenuous exercise.

Limbering his arms and legs, he stood before the long sheet of mirrored glass he had installed in the garage for the purpose of gauging the tone and bulk of his musculature. Pretty damn all right for a man nearly forty-five, he told himself in pride. Gray might show in his hair, but his body was the body of a man fifteen years younger.

God knows he had paid his dues for that flat, taut belly, the long and sturdy legs, the spring in his step. Something in him refused to yield to the encroachment of middle age, would not tolerate the flabbiness of sedentary living.

He gazed fondly at his mirrored crotch, cock and balls delineated in length and heft. He was, in his secret heart, a cock-proud man; he didn't down-mouth himself for it, either. Body-proud, also; and, since a man's sexual apparatus is the primary focus of a man's physical being, why should he not be proud of his cock?

He could feel the seriousness of exercise settling into his being. He could snatch only half an hour with the weights every morning before work; Thursday afternoon was the time for the Thursday Man, when he could work through a schedule of lifting with attention to the detail of sensation and accomplishment, the complete repertoire of muscle toning.

He began slowly, working with concentration, feeling his body shaping toward the lifting of increasing weights in a meticulous pattern of preparation for an ultimate effort in which he would strive to go beyond the highest point of effort he had previously achieved.

Almost sensuously he built the tension of performance, aware of oxygen expanding his lungs, enjoying the run of sweat on his skin, feeling the litheness of youth returning

7

in the play of his muscles. He would be good today, very good; indeed, when he went into the big lift, he performed without strain, achieving easily a greater weight than he had ever lifted before.

He let the bar drop and stood panting, hands stroking the sweaty bellows of his chest muscles as he eased his shoulders to work out the poisons of fatigue. Without moving from before the revealing glass, he dropped the sweaty shorts and placed a hand on his cock, watching as the warm stroke of his palm brought it instantly to an alert stance.

For a lustful instant, he almost wished that Eleanor was here; the sight of him, so virile and young, would put the response in her flesh which he still delighted to arouse in her. But the pattern of their sex life reserved such connubial pleasures for Sunday night.

One night a week was enough; he fucked for her pleasure far more than for his own. He was, he knew smugly, a good husband, pleasing himself by pleasing her, though her stomach was too soft and she no longer possessed the female strength and heat of their young days.

A moment only of self-gratification, more an accolade to his flesh than a satisfaction; he put on the fresh shorts, along with the T-shirt. Hitting the button to open the garage door, he wheeled out the bicycle, pausing briefly before departure to apply a gauge to check the pressures. He had pumped up the tires this morning in preparation, so they were right. The garage door secured, he mounted in a fluid motion and pedaled off on his solitary trek.

In the subdivision surrounding his home, he concentrated on the pedaling—feeling the strain on his legs as he crested each hill, enjoying the rush of the down-ride, shifting gears as required—letting the work of bicycling ease him off from the more strenuous weight lifting. At first an occasional car passed, one way or the other; once a teen-ager leaned out the window, shouting derisively.

Soon enough, however, all traffic had vanished and he was truly alone in the world of the Thursday Man. In the open countryside, he slowed his speed, sitting back in the saddle with one hand on the handlebars, pedaling leisurely along the deserted black-topped road. He took each juncture at random, for he never went the same way twice. It was all a traveling into the solitude of himself.

He had achieved that state in which physical action was disengaged from his mind; and so he dreamed again of the hermitage that was his, up there alone on the lake.

Of the hermitage that *would* be.

His mind, his being, had shifted imperceptibly into the future of himself, when he would be only *Him*, the cabin, the redwood post-and-beam bachelor place he wanted so badly.

When he knew it was impossible, now and forever.

Post-and-beam, built all of redwood, with a great sun deck; the enormous living room glassed on one side, making the marvelous view an integral part of the establishment. It was possible, of course, in the context of his financial standing. If he really wanted to, he could replace, this year or next, the shabby little place of family vacations.

But why do it? he considered sadly—when never in this life would it be possible to free himself of all the encumbrances of possession and responsibility, to become the *Him* he yearned to be. Pedaling slowly, he yielded himself to the impossible daydream.

The girls . . . yes, the girls. Three of them now, alive in his mind, warm girls, girls with passion and love in their elegant bodies, along with a freedom of the flesh he himself now owned.

This weekend, however, it is a new girl. He was expecting Gloria, the redhead; instead, to his delight and surprise, when Gloria's red sports car sputters to a stop in the parking area, a strange woman reigns behind the wheel.

Coming out on the sun deck to greet his weekend housemate, he stops short in surprise.

"Hello," she says, smiling up at him. In her voice, beyond a wary curiosity, he can detect a tentative appreciation of his appearance.

"Well, hello," he replies. "Who are you?"

She gets out, reaches into the back seat for a Vuitton

weekend bag. Swinging it at the length of an arm, she comes toward him slowly over the spaced round stones that make a pathway to his door.

This one has black hair, true and glossy, with black eyebrows heavier than a girl usually allows herself. Enticing legs, and she is wearing white silk slacks and a white silk blouse that reveals the ampleness of her breasts.

She pauses before the steps, still gazing up at him where he stands with spread legs, hands on hips. He is dressed in white, also; baggy white pants and a flowing white shirt, almost a karate outfit. It feels loose and good on him.

"Gloria sent me," she says simply. "I'm Marti."

"Why didn't Gloria come herself?"

Her eyes shift, but only momentarily; she regards him again with that still, speculative gaze.

"Because she said I'd enjoy a weekend on your lake."

The words are almost indifferent in their context of sexual meaning. He can only smile and say, "Now, why would Gloria do a thing like that?"

She comes on up the steps, to stand close enough for him to catch a faint whiff of perfume. "Oh, Gloria and I are best friends," she says, laughing conspiratorially. "When she couldn't come herself, she insisted I take her place."

"Nice of her," he says noncommittally. "Why couldn't she come?"

"Her father's in the hospital. Nothing serious, but she felt she really ought to stay in town." Her chuckle is a low-throated, friendly sound. "She said a man like you doesn't deserve to waste a weekend by himself just because a girl's father happens to be in the hospital."

He is examining, behind the conversation, his feelings in the matter. He has, unconsciously, counted on Gloria—it is her time and her turn—and so, despite himself, he feels deprived. Yet a new girl, untested, untried . . .

"Why did you decide to accept Gloria's invitation?"

Her gaze is frank in surveying him. "Because Gloria's told me a hundred times that you're a nice man . . . and all man." She chuckles again. "In fact, Gloria gives quite a heated description of you in the sack."

10

He tries to accept the statement in the casual manner in which it has been made. "That's nice of her, I must say."

Her gaze is still honest, still open. "Of course I'm not all that sure I'm going to fuck you. I do hope you understand that."

Charmed by the plain statement, he answers with the same candor: "In that case, we'll simply have a nice weekend together. What would you like to do?"

Truly—somewhat to his surprise—he has experienced no great sense of disappointment. This Marti, he knows without thinking, must be accepted on her own terms. It would be entirely wrong to pressure her to yield him the use of her body. Indeed, he reflects, it would be a delightful experience to share a weekend with a woman without sharing also the flesh, the hours quickened by the delightful tension of passion acknowledged yet denied.

She swings the weekend case back and forth. "First of all, I insist on the grand tour of this fabulous place . . . Gloria talks about it as much as she talks about you. Then, before lunch, I'd love a swim. And, naturally, I expect your famous Eggs Colony for lunch."

"Gloria did give you a detailed rundown, didn't she?" he remarks, feeling pleased. "Eggs Colony it shall be. And everything else your heart desires."

He shows her first the guest bedroom, where each of the girls stays in her turn. Even in this he maintains his solitude, using his own great bed for sex, not for sleeping together. As invariably, on Monday morning, he sends them away so he can have the week for himself alone.

After she has dropped her bag on the bed, he gives her the tour: the small kitchen, impeccable with its copper-toned surfaces, the compact Jenn-Air range with its grill top, the large refrigerator with the ice maker in the door. She loves the great living room with its stone fireplace ("It must be lovely on winter nights.") and his own bedroom with its wide view out over the lake.

She gives him a sly look out of the corner of her eye. "That beautiful bed certainly is made for romping. How big is it, about half an acre?"

11

It is the only antique in the place, bigger than king size, with a hand-carved headboard and footboard—solid enough, he knows from experience, to stand all degrees of thumpings and racketings around. A firm mattress too, very firm. He hates soft mattresses.

He laughs. "Big enough to have fun in, small enough to find a body in when a man's got the need."

"I think I'll get my bathing suit and go swimming," she declares, deftly avoiding the implied invitation.

"Bathing suits are outlawed here at The Aerie," he informs her solemnly.

"The Aerie," she says musingly. "That means 'Eagle's Nest,' doesn't it?" She regards him again. "Are you an eagle?"

"If I were a bird, I'd be an eagle," he tells her boldly.

She continues to regard him for a still moment. Then, abruptly, she turns away. "All right, if you say so. I'll be back."

She disappears into the guest bedroom, to return almost immediately in the naked flesh. He looks upon her with frank appraisal while, with a mock pose, she withstands his encompassing gaze.

She is slender with her tallness, but with surprisingly ripe breasts. A lovely, slim-lined belly slopes seductively into the heavy black thatch covering a prominent mount. There is the blemish of an appendectomy scar on her creamy white flesh; otherwise, she is perfect.

"Seen enough?" she asks challengingly. Then: "It's not exactly fair, keeping your clothes on while a girl stands naked."

Laughing, he unbelts the slacks and steps out of them, pulls the loose shirt over his head and tosses it into a chair. With gratification, a surge of desire, he hears her tiny gasp. Every woman he has ever known has gasped at first sight of his cock. He is pleased that, despite the stirrings of lust, it betrays not the least hint of an erection. An erection is not demanded or expected at this stage in their budding relationship.

"Shall we go swimming?" he inquires.

"*Let's go swimming!*" she says gaily, moving past him down the steps toward the lake yonder beyond the trees. On the way, however, slowing to match his step, she takes his hand, swinging their arms happily as they tramp down the steep grade. For the last few yards she abandons him, running out onto the wooden dock. But he calls, "*Wait a minute,*" and she halts, poised in inquiry.

"*Get in the boat.*" He grins at her. "*I'll take you to my secret swimming hole.*"

"*Oh, wonderful!*" she exclaims, clambering into the sleek runabout without waiting for assistance.

It is a small white-sand beach, a mile down the lake, hidden at the head of a cove where a small creek flows in. He runs the boat gently up on the sand, takes out a line to tie to a sapling. He straightens, to watch her poised momentarily, arms raised, before she flips suddenly over the side. In the shallow dive, her body turns into a lovely arrow of flesh in the dappled sunlight. Hurrying aboard, he follows suit, surfacing within arm's reach. They tread water, grinning at each other in mutual delight.

He is moved to confession. "*I've never brought anyone here. Not Gloria . . . no one.*"

Her eyes catch his, hold them. "*Why me, then?*"

"*I don't know.*"

She turns away, swimming strongly with the first stroke, to go straight out into the lake. She is a good swimmer, her slim body knifing through the water with the sleek efficiency of a seal. He stands on the bottom, sand grainy against the soles of his feet, to watch until at last she consents to return. She stops her momentum with a hand on his shoulder—the first time, except in holding hands down the steep path, she has touched him.

They swim separately, coming together at intervals to romp like teen-agers, splashing water, each striving in laughter to duck the other, until their bodies are pleasantly water-logged. Only once does he actually touch her flesh; he slides one hand down the length of her back as she swims by, his palm alive to the smooth texture of her skin, the

13

sweet hump of her ass. He can feel the power of the long legs as she flutter-kicks in laughing escape.

After they return to The Aerie, she keeps him company in the kitchen while he expertly prepares Eggs Colony and English muffins dripping with pure honey. At the table on the sun deck, shaded by a striped umbrella, they eat hungrily. Finished, Marti helps him carry the dishes to the kitchen, rinse them, stow them in the dishwasher.

Then, she stretches languorously, remarking, "I hope you don't mind if a girl takes a long, long nap. Because that's exactly what I feel like now."

"I enjoy a nap myself," he admits, so they part, each going to separate bedrooms.

He takes a shower, stretches cool and clean on top of the sheet. In two minutes, he is asleep. He awakes, an unknown time later, to a drowsy awareness of her presence. He does not stir, but waits upon her intent.

She hovers beside the bed; he knows that she is gazing upon his nakedness. After a suspenseful moment, her hand warmly cups his balls, making his cock, slowly and surely, begin to rise. When it has demonstrated sufficient interest, her hand slips up to stroke the throbbing stalk with sensuous firmness.

His hips respond, rising, but she whispers, "Don't move, my eagle. Don't move."

He gives himself over to her. She leans over his thighs, the long wings of her black hair brushing his skin, and takes his cock sweetly into her warm mouth. Deliberately her lips slide gently down the length of the shaft; then, as slowly, upward again. It is a deep gulping, a swallowing, that brings his cock to a throbbing edge of desire. He can no longer hold himself in restraint. But again she commands, "Don't move, not yet."

He waits, with what patience he can muster, until she straddles his loins, easing the warm, wet lips of her pussy sweetly over the greedy head. She holds herself poised, only the pulsing head penetrating her maw, moving up and down in a tantalizing stroke that makes him want to scream with desire.

14

On the very edge of unbearable frustration, in one complex thrust of her jewel-jointed hips, she takes in completely the rampant, straining cock. She sighs with fulfillment as, with strong arms, he turns her underneath. He gazes into her startled eyes as she bucks into orgasm with the first full stroke of his cock . . .

There was suddenly the huge station wagon, utterly unexpected in this desolate stretch of road, looming up behind him as the bicycle wobbled out into its path. He shouted, his voice drowned in the crash of metal against metal. His head spinning, he pitched off the bike, slamming with force against the ground. He tumbled into the willowed ditch, the sharp stabs of pain in his legs driving away the cloudy dream of fucking beautiful Marti in The Aerie.

The Woman:

She watched him scrambling out of the low willows growing thickly in the road ditch, moving so painfully, so slowly, it put her heart into her throat.

Oh, my God, I ran over him, her mind screamed, visualizing instantly the swarming of the police, the ruthless interrogation—and how in the world could she explain her presence on this deserted country road when she herself did not know how she came to be here? Wallowing shamelessly in a lustful daydream, she must have been driving at random. Her loins were still warm and wet in response to her fantasy of the telephone man in his heavy tool belt and tight blue jeans.

Her instinctive reaction was to flee the scene, hoping her victim was too rattled to take note of the license plate. Her foot was ready on the accelerator—when she saw the blood on his legs. Leaving the motor running, though automatically slamming the gear into *park*, she fled from behind the wheel.

When she reached him, she gasped, "Are you hurt? Please tell me you're not hurt."

The man rose tall, nearly naked, before her. Gingerly he lifted each leg, testing for locomotion. He tried each set of muscles in his body in turn, moving his shoulders separately, then the neck muscles.

He looked at her, then, for the first time. The pale blue T-shirt, she noted irrelevantly, was ripped, exposing a hairy chest. His voice was sour. "I seem to be in one piece. Through no fault of yours."

"But you veered in front of me!" she said, switching from panic to indignation.

"Listen, lady, you weren't driving exactly a straight line yourself," he said, his attack matching her own aggressive defense. "You haven't been drinking, have you?"

"Of course not!" she exclaimed angrily. Then, apprehensively: "But you're bleeding. Are you *sure* you're all right?"

He looked down at his legs. "So I am," he said in mild surprise.

Both cuts were on his left leg, one high on the inside of his thigh, the other deep across the shin. They were seeping blood, staining his leg.

"There's a first-aid kit in the car." With something to do, she was surer of herself. "Come around here so I can patch you up." She got the small kit out of the glove compartment and returned. "Up on the fender," she ordered.

Obediently he took a perch on the front fender. She opened the kit with shaking fingers, and found a folded bandage and a small bottle of alcohol. Kneeling, she swabbed away the blood and the dirt.

"The trouble with you automobile drivers, a bicycle doesn't exist," he said as though he never deigned to drive a car. "You don't even *see* a bicycle."

She looked up into his face. "I'm sorry," she said sincerely. "I was . . . I guess I was just daydr . . . woolgathering." She made a small laugh. "I don't even know what I'm *doing* on this road. I was on the way home from the grocery store."

He gazed down on her, looking strangely uncertain . . . even guilty, she thought. "Do you do that, too? Daydream, I mean?"

"I'm afraid so," she said honestly. "Too much."

He bit his lip, looked away. "I guess I was gathering my share of the wool, too. Just pedaling along there, my mind a thousand miles away." His voice gathered strength. "So I don't suppose the accident is anybody's fault . . . not if it's *both* our fault."

Her hand, ceasing the swabbing motion, lingered on his leg. "Thank you," she said. Flustered by the sensation of his hairiness, she began again, more vigorously, to cleanse the area. He flinched and jerked away as she raked heedlessly across the area of abrasion.

"Hold on," she said, grasping the muscular calf in her

17

other hand. "Only a moment more. If the dirt's left in there . . ."

As firmly as if he were a bruised child, she cleaned away the road grit embedded in his broken skin, making it bleed more freely. Twice he jerked his leg away, but she held fast. She finished the job with firmly efficient hands, applying antiseptic and a pad of bandage, taping it down with adhesive.

"Now," she said in triumph. "That takes care of *that*."

She stood up, preparing to doctor the place on the inside of his thigh. Suddenly aware of his crotch, so plainly delineated in the tight shorts, she became self-conscious.

"This one looks like it's cut even worse," she said in a flustered voice.

"Be careful then," he admonished. With gingerly touches, she swabbed away the blood. He was hairy even here, the growth longer and finer on the inside of his thigh. Involuntarily she thought of it growing up under the shorts, merging with the hair around . . .

Her hands began to tremble. His flesh was too intimate, too real; she was afraid of an irresistible urge to touch his bird, so enticingly outlined under the light blue fabric. She had never done such a thing in her life; never even *thought* about actually touching a man . . . except in fantasy, when she could safely dare anything.

Afraid that she was blushing, she had to look into his face to see if he had noticed. He was watching her; she saw how uneasy—almost anticipatory—his smile was.

"You're good at this," he remarked.

"With twin girls, I've had my share of practice," she said sharply.

"You've got twins? So have I. Except mine are boys."

"Well, *that's* strange, isn't it?"

She was deeply grateful for this diversion of her dangerous thoughts. Feelings, only *feelings*, she assured herself, because of course I would never do such a thing as actually touch him. Actually open the door to an Adventure. After all, Adventures happened only inside her head. Adventures were unreal, *had* to be unreal, daydreams of the possible instead of the possibility.

"How old are yours?"

"Twelve," he said.

"Why, so are mine! What month were they born?"

"October. October the twentieth, to be exact."

She leaned back. "*Why, that is unbelievable.*"

"You don't mean to say . . . ?"

She nodded, thinking involuntarily: In the cold January of that year, the coldest January I can remember, *he* turned under the covers to the woman his wife, *he* entered her, giving her not one child but two, and surely it was the same night, maybe the very same *time* of night, as when Hale turned to me under the covers because of course the furnace wasn't working and it was cold, so cold, but the love-making made us warm and cozy and I couldn't bring myself to make him get out of me immediately, and so I got the twins . . .

The man was looking at her and, as real as if he had spoken, she knew he was thinking the same thought, living the same realization.

Betrayed by the renewed suffusion of blood into her face, she knew guiltily that, down there, her nest was warm again, as warm as when the telephone man had been just ready to stab her to the quick . . .

"Well, that *is* a coincidence," she said rapidly, denying it because she *had* to deny it. She hid her face by bending her head to concentrate with tender ferocity on the cut in his flesh.

Willing her fingers not to tremble, she spread open the cut, making sure it was clean. "I don't think it'll need to be stitched," she said doubtfully. "One stitch, maybe, or two, to keep from making a scar."

She used a large Band-Aid this time, applying it carefully to hold together the lips of the wound. She had to press firmly, both hands between his legs. She was sharply aware of the hairy tickle of sensation on the back of one hand.

"There, now," she said, as she would have spoken to a child.

19

He responded, smiling, to the tone. "Mama has made it all well." Sliding down from the fender, he asked curiously, "Do you come this way often?"

"I told you," she said quickly. "Never."

He laughed. "Just wanted to make sure, so I could watch out. Get off into the ditch, or something, whenever I saw you coming."

Feeling relief, she laughed with him. She was aware of him as a person now, not simply the victim of her carelessness. He was tall and he looked very strong, athletic, with the taut, hard muscles of a young man though there was gray in his hair. Hale, her husband, had always been soft-fleshed, chubby, even in his high-school football days.

This man had a lean and handsome face, with strong, flat planes and a noble nose. A man with obvious respect for his body, who took care of himself; even if he did wear his bicycling shorts so snug it was practically indecent. Of course, she reminded herself practically, he didn't exactly expect to run into a woman out here on this deserted road. *Literally* run into her.

She had to stop the thinking again. She turned her head, saying, "What about your bike? Is it . . . ?"

"I guess I'd better check."

He moved away from the too-near nearness, stooping to lift the bike and roll it back and forth. The front wheel wobbled precariously.

"I guess I'll have to push it," he said ruefully.

"Put it in the station wagon," she urged. "I'll run you home."

"Oh, that's too much trouble."

"I've caused *you* trouble, haven't I?"

"OK, I guess so," he said, conceding the point. "It *would* be a pretty long walk."

She gave him the keys so he could unlock the rear door, watched as he moved the grocery sacks to one side so he could insert the bicycle. She slid behind the wheel as he came around and got in on the other side.

"You'll have to show me the way," she said as she started the motor.

It was necessary to continue a short distance down the road before finding a turn-around. Inexplicably, she was driving slowly, as though to stretch out the time they would be together in the air-conditioned intimacy of the station wagon.

After a silence, he asked, "By the way, what's your name?" and told her his own after her reply.

There didn't seem to be anything more to say along that line, so he remarked, chuckling, "That sure is strange, our kids being exactly the same age."

"Do you have any others, besides the twin boys?"

"No. There was a good chance they'd be twins again, and we didn't want . . ." He paused, chuckling again. "It sure wouldn't do for me and you to make a baby together. They'd be twins sure as hell, wouldn't they?"

She could find no reply to that provocative statement. Already, in spite of the slow driving, they were again within the city limits, with houses clustering closer together. Soon now, she knew, he would say, "This is it," and that *would* be it.

She didn't know—didn't *want* to know—exactly what she was trying to hang on to, stretch out, extend into . . . into what? She didn't want to know that, either.

He directed her, directed her again, and there was nothing to talk about any more because every line of conversation seemed to lead into . . . into what, she didn't know.

He sat sprawled loosely beside her, legs open, the way a good athlete sits in complete relaxation. She remained aware of his body, she decided, because he was himself so acutely aware of it.

He's probably on the prowl, she decided abruptly. I'm just too inexperienced to recognize it. Probably sees every woman as an easy lay, been unfaithful to his wife a dozen times, because, when a man's looking, occasionally he'll find. A man like him, so body-proud, one woman couldn't

21

satisfy his need. Obviously he worked hard to keep himself in such beautiful shape at his age.

Oh, she'd had passes made at her. But the man always seemed to have to get half-drunk first. She knew how cool and aloof she could seem, as though, in social situations, her mind, her feelings, were off somewhere in a world of their own. As, indeed, they often were. She had never been tempted because those pawing, fumbling men had seemed in such jarring dissonance with her secret dreams of a sexual encounter that would be an Adventure.

"Stop here," he said abruptly. She pulled to the curb, looking at the white colonial. "Is this your house?"

He was embarrassed. "Well, no. We're nearly there, though, and I'd rather . . ."

She gazed at him steadily, with a faint smile. "You'd just rather not be fetched home by another woman."

"Well, yeah." He laughed a short laugh. "I don't intend to try to explain the accident. Much less *you*."

The first hint of conspiracy between them; but, of course, she realized he was right. She wouldn't have wanted to bring this man home to Hale, either. With or without an explanation.

"I understand," she said almost tenderly, out of the sadness that it was ending. Even this little Adventure, which had been merely speculation, nothing more.

He didn't move to open the car door. Perhaps he didn't want it to end, either. Whatever *it* was.

"Well. I hope I'll run into you again sometime." A chuckle. "Though not exactly in the same way."

No answer, because any possible answer would be too dangerous. "Have you lived here long?"

"All my life. I was born here."

"So was I."

A silence, as they mutually contemplated these twin facts. Then he said, "How is it that we've never met?"

"Well, it *is* a city," she said, almost defensively. "Maybe not the *biggest* city in the world, but . . . Where did you go to school?"

He told her, and she told him: different schools, but not all that far apart. Both were in the best part of town.

"We must have been at many of the same football games," he said thoughtfully. "Of course, you'd have been a few years behind me."

"Thank you," she said, too archly. Then she added unnecessarily, "I was cheerleader, *head* cheerleader, my senior year."

"I'm sure I must have seen you, then, because I used to go to games after I graduated—even after I finished college. Still do, sometimes, as a matter of fact. And our schools played a schedule together."

"But I'm not head cheerleader anymore," she said with a quiet laugh. "This is getting to be a silly sort of talking, don't you think?"

It made a silence. Abruptly, with a jerky movement of his bare legs, he said, "Will you . . . take that country road again, sometime . . . on a Thursday?"

There it was.

He had to be what used to be called a "wolf." Lying in wait for an unwary Red Riding Hood walking innocently to Grandma's house with all her little goodies warm in her little basket.

"I don't know," she said soberly. "I really don't know."

She was looking directly into his eyes, as he was looking into hers. Their gaze held and clung for a breathless moment. Then he was out of the station wagon, getting his bicycle out, going up the street, pushing the damaged machine. His strong legs were sturdy in climbing the hill. She had never liked men with a lot of hair. Only Billy-Bob, that first one, had had such a heavy pelt . . .

She did not move to start the engine until, without looking back, he had gone out of sight over the crest.

The Man:

He managed to keep her out of his head until bedtime. First, he concentrated on getting the damaged bicycle into the garage—and himself out of the torn T-shirt and dirt-smeared shorts—without notice. Why, exactly, he did not analyze.

That small conspiracy accomplished, he absorbed himself in the evening news until dinner. Eleanor happily filled the togetherness of eating with a detailed description of her duplicate-bridge triumph of the afternoon.

There were also the boys, of course, Eric and Steve; he stared at them thoughtfully across the table, thinking about those twin girls somewhere across town who had been hotly conceived on that same cold January night in 1969. That time, so early in his marriage to Eleanor, seemed too long ago to result in these great lumps of boy-flesh sitting at his table, their heads filled with nothing but the football camp they'd be going off to on Monday.

Television afterward, though he seldom watched television except for sports; so only at bedtime did she steal back into his mind. He tried to fight her off by putting in her place the unfinished business of the imaginary Marti, hovering hot-bottomed over his cock up there at The Aerie, sliding down over him, taking him deep . . .

He could not conjure Marti. Clinging stubbornly to her place in his mind was the real woman who had so disastrously broken into his daydream with her great clumsy station wagon. Who drove those gas guzzlers any more, anyway?

She had responded to him.

Her fingers had actually trembled, touching him on the tender inside of his thigh, where the worst cut had been. She had stared openly at his cock revealed by the pale blue shorts. His weapon, aware of the attention, had stirred; and

24

surely she had marked the awakening, she had felt it as he had felt it.

A damned good-looking woman, older though she was than the free-spirited girls of his dreams. And married. A remote kind of beauty that made a man want to reach out and get behind it, find the woman waiting inside that delicate, chiseled loveliness—the warm woman with secret desires of her own. That was an expensive linen dress she had been wearing, white and gold. Had he been right in thinking that she was naked underneath it?

And had she not confessed to daydreaming of sex, as he had been dreaming? She had seemed somehow, to his awakening male instincts, like a woman disturbed in the middle of a good fuck.

He could see why she'd have been head cheerleader in high school. That slim body, with the tight little pears of breasts and the long legs, must have been ravishing in a cheerleader's innocently revealing costume. Probably had all the guys panting after her, too; bird dogs trailing a bitch in heat. She wouldn't have given in, though—oh, maybe once or twice, but only to satisfy her own hungers, not those of an importunate boy—because she would have been cool and far-off even then. It was a part of her nature. It would take a real man to get inside her.

He had got inside her today.

Not in actuality, of course. But, figuratively speaking, he had laid her down on the station-wagon seat, lifted her dress to expose her naked body underneath, had inserted the old cock right where it counted.

Except—even when he had invited her to meet him again, he had sensed his own reluctance.

His life was all right. He had duties and responsibilities, true; but also his freedoms and solitudes. Why risk upsetting all that *now*, when he had never done so? Yet—he *had* asked her to see him again; and, her eyes direct and serious, she had replied with a beautiful honesty, "I don't know. I really don't know."

He snugged down into the bed, knowing smugly that not

once since Eleanor had married him had he betrayed her; he had kept the bargain of their lives.

Yes. Eleanor had married *him*. Those years ago, she had made a dead-set assault on his bachelorhood . . . and she had won. He had not been unhappy in his working-bachelor existence; even if, in consideration of his planned banking career, it was necessary to be discreet. But with his nifty little apartment that would now be called a "pad," with his standing in the community as a rising man in the banking fraternity, with his Harvard MBA behind him, there had been girls aplenty. It would, he reflected with a secret glee, surprise some of the people in this town who *some* of those girls had been.

Eleanor, daughter of a founding family even older in the community than his, had not been among them. Eleanor had appeared one night at one of the small parties he gave periodically. Sitting watchfully in a corner, she had noted —she told him later—how every girl in the room was acutely aware of him. So she had decided that, to be different from every other woman in the city, she would simply have to become his wife.

The next day, a Sunday, she returned to the apartment early enough to wake him out of a late sleep. She had not come to be fucked as, naturally, he had assumed; indeed, they did not make real love until the wedding night.

She came, instead, to tell him frankly that she loved him and meant to marry him, even if she was older by a couple of years. When he had taken this, also, as an invitation to bed, she rapidly disabused him of the notion.

Not that she was cold. Quite gladly, sitting fully clothed on the floor between his pajama-clad legs, she had sucked him off—the first woman who had ever put her mouth on him. He came so quickly that she was forced to swallow it all. But she came up smiling, laying her loving head on his crotch, cherishing him.

Eleanor was, after all, a nice girl of good family who would surely make a marvelous wife for a man with his ambitions; besides, he became utterly addicted to her doing him with her expert mouth. So the fact that her father was president of the bank where he worked scarcely figured into his calculated consent to marriage.

On their wedding night he discovered, to his astonishment, that she was virgin.

There on the side of the road today, it could have gone like that, also. There had certainly been the moment when *she* had looked at his cock so hungrily he had had the unassailable feeling that in the next minute she was going to touch him with a bold hand.

That should have been the way of it. She should have touched him, not lightly, but with a bold grasp, shaping it long and strong in her hand through the thin cloth. Then, right there beside the road, she should have pulled the zipper and taken it into her mouth, sucking him off with all the passion hidden inside that cool beauty of hers.

He put a hand under the covers to touch the nakedness of himself. He had half a hard-on just from thinking about *her*. He gripped himself, imagining it to be *her* hand . . . and then, again, her mouth.

Yes. She had to come to him next Thursday. *She had to*.

Until the boys had been born, Eleanor had shown herself to be insanely jealous. She knew how long he had been a bachelor; five years in this city after Harvard Business School, with never a thought of marriage. For years she had watched him like a hawk, acutely aware every time a woman's head turned, an eye gleamed, a smile beckoned. Each time, she was convinced that the woman was a conquest from his halcyon days, pantingly ruthless to take him again though he was now a respectable married man.

Because of her painful jealousy, if for no other reason, he had kept their bargain. Simply because it had meant so much to her.

Did it really mean that much anymore? He wondered. Eleanor seemed smugly content with her life of bridge with other expert players, their assured status in the social and business life of this small city, and with their safe and confident sex on Sunday nights. Always on Sunday.

How long had it been since she had volunteered to suck him off?

Holding himself, speaking quietly into darkness, he said, "Eleanor. Do me."

She groaned and stirred in response to the marriage-hallowed summons. He held still, silent and waiting. She stirred again, more reluctantly; then her voice, blurred with sleep, "Do you *have* to have it? I'm so sleepy, I . . ."

"I don't *have* to have it," he said in the resigned tone that, he knew, would command obedience. A long time since he had asked her, and then only as a part of the Sunday-night ritual.

The more she hesitated, the more he desired it. He kept the demanding silence strong between them until at last, with a final yielding groan, she rolled over to him, her head burrowing under the sheet and into his waiting groin.

Her warm hand first, holding ready the half-hardness for her mouth's seeking; the most beautiful mouth in the world for this lovely doing, strong and tender at once, infinitely inventive. Half-asleep, she began slowly, but there was that in Eleanor's nature which could not refuse her talent.

He did not put his hands to her head, working so sweetly above his loins, but relaxed into the pillow, yielding only his cock to her, freeing the rest of himself for . . .

That cool beauty. She, too, must have a beautiful mouth; she'd have to, with that intense yearning to taste him, savor him, swallow him whole. She could have done it today, so easily . . .

Groaning, he began to come, starting with a sensuous slowness in his melting spine but then gushing out as he felt Eleanor drinking deeply of his essence. Only when it was finished did he touch her, to cuddle her head into his loins for a contented minute.

She raised up. "All right?"

"Thank you, dear."

She went away to her side of the bed, leaving him in his

solitude of completion. He sought sleep hungrily, for somewhere inside him was a tiny knot of shame.

Never until now in their life together had he put the dream of another woman between himself and Eleanor's mouth.

The Woman:

It was different with her; *he* stayed with her all the way to bedtime. Not the good body, not even the pale blue crotch she had been so intensely aware of; but those parting words, "Will you . . . take that country road again sometime . . . on a Thursday?"

The question had laid it squarely into her hot little lap. The idea remained with her, as warm as a touching hand. She could, for once in her life, have a real Adventure. Except . . . She shuddered deep inside; except, in a *real* Adventure, she would not have the control she enjoyed in her erotic reveries. In her mind, like running a film backward to start over again, she often altered a sequence, or terminated it at any point satisfactory to her soul and to her flesh.

But . . . *real*? Some other person, with his own demands and desires? And, degrading thought: Would she be only one more scalp for his tepee pole? Both attracted and repelled, she shivered again.

She had always counted herself as someone special. Except for that one time—the first time. A coldness congealed in her loins; this man, also, was hairy—nearly as hairy as Billy-Bob. She had *never* been sexually attracted to hairy men.

He continued to walk in her thoughts as she dealt with putting away the groceries and, eventually, with cooking dinner—so much easier now that the girls were off at camp —and eating it with Hale at the other end of the table. Thank goodness, Hale, as usual, had brought briefs from his law office to study at a card table before the television set, allowing her to retire alone into the bedroom.

She put on her filmiest nightgown, loving the silken texture sliding slickly cool down her thighs, and got into bed. She looked up at the ceiling, hands resting lightly on the inside of her thighs, knowing already that tonight she would masturbate.

She was feeling around in her mind for a fantasy. She found only *him*. It had never been anyone real before, not even a movie star, a notorious singer of songs. She had always created her imaginary men out of the whole cloth of her need; younger, with dark, smooth skin and muscular asses.

He was at least ten years older, despite the well-tended body . . . and *hairy*. His bird must be *huge*, the way it bulged under those pale blue shorts. Had it *jerked*, that time she had stared at it? *Yes. It had definitely moved*.

Delicately she touched her nest, not yet initiating the twirling motion that always brought her swiftly to climax. She didn't want it to happen too quickly. But . . . the disturbing reality of this man in her mind, so tall, so strong, so nearly naked, brought a sharp focus to her sensations. It made his image as sharp and real as if he were in the bed beside her, *his* hand on her throbbing nest.

She began to pant in short gasps of desire. She could have done it. With him balanced on the fender, she could have reached boldly for the zipper, freeing his bird to her hand. Because of course he had been naked underneath, as she had been naked today, as if in fated preparation for the accidental meeting. She could have taken him standing up, walking hard into him, feeling him sliding down from the fender to take her as their bodies merged.

She was panting hard now, her finger twirling feverishly as, against her will, her thinking—dreaming—shifted from Today to Next Thursday. It was just as possible next week, wasn't it? Meet him on that lonely stretch of road, make him lie down helpless on the station-wagon seat while she came over him, raping him of his hardness with the ruthless thrusting of her hips.

Her breathing slowed as she subsided out of orgasm. In her heated senses, still in mental orgasm with the fantasy-so-real of taking him in a manner she had never practiced with any man, the darkened room was a hothouse of desire.

31

God! she thought. Oh, God, if it could only *be* like that . . .

Yet, underneath, she was uneasy. She had lost control; there at the end, fantasy had bridged into a species of reality, as though she were now somehow committed to Next Thursday. Committed to fucking *him*. Her mind shuddered under the impact of that uncompromising word; she had never before thought it so graphically in the secret reaches of her womanly mind.

She was still wide awake when Hale entered the room, turning on his bedside lamp to light his way into the bathroom. Her heart sank when she saw him emerge wearing only his pajama top—his signal that tonight he desired sex.

A stout boy in high school, he was now a plump man, though, weather permitting, he played golf regularly. With short, sturdy legs and a hefty barrel, Hale still carried strength beneath the plumpness, for in high school he had been an all-district fullback. Indeed, several colleges had offered him athletic scholarships but, for a reason she had never known, he had not played college ball.

She had never accustomed her husband to an occasional denial of her flesh. Because of her gratitude that Hale had consented to marry her even after the episode of Billy-Bob Radley, the pattern had been established in their first days of marriage.

She waited patiently for his plump hand reaching to explore her nest, knowing that tonight of all nights, despite her bone-deep reluctance, she could not risk denying him. To deny Hale would, after all, be a self-admission that the allegiance of her body had fled to another man.

Obediently she touched him as he touched her, making a ring of thumb and forefinger for a wifely arousal of his limp bird. She knew the ritual step by step; Hale followed the same pattern every time until at last he came over her and humped for four minutes before reaching release. She knew it was exactly four minutes; more than once she had counted off the seconds in her mind to avoid a disappointment of her own flesh.

Sometimes, out of sheer familiarity with his unvarying pace, she also reached a desperately strained orgasm. More often not; but it had not seemed to matter that much. Her rich fantasy life more than satisfied her needs.

She opened her legs when he was ready to settle his plump belly on her belly. She remained unstirred, lying passively under his diligent pumping as he launched into his four-minute mile.

She had started going steady with Hale in the ninth grade. He was, quite simply, the first boy to ask her for a date. In those years when going steady was the established norm, no one had ever tried to cut in, though twice she had been voted most popular girl, and, in her senior year, had become head cheerleader. She was considered Hale's property, as Hale was contentedly hers.

In those safe, secure years, she had lived a secure social and sex life. Never a need to worry about a prom date, because there was always Hale. Their intricate petting was apportioned on a precise scale of increasing complexity, from the first kiss through the first fumbling touch of his hand on her clothed breast to . . . well, it was designed, quite without conversation or agreement, to culminate on their foreordained wedding night.

On the night in their senior year when he had scored the winning touchdown—she remembered abruptly—for the first time she had brought him off with her hand. Afterward, they had solemnly discussed setting the wedding date, apparently necessary now that an acknowledged gush of male semen had occurred in her virgin presence.

The sexual thinking warm in her mind, she was beginning to feel something. Counting herself safely back in that old time instead of dwelling on the man she had met today, she turned her attention to Hale's physical penetration, shifting under him to take him deeper. She had been afraid, she realized guiltily, that *his* proud bird might stand erect in her mind even as Hale performed husbandly love.

"The olden time," as her children called it. So safe, so secure, so certain that everything would work out for the best of all possible worlds.

That spring, with graduation hovering over their heads, she and Hale had already decided to get married in June and go off together to college; that would make college as safe and secure as high school had been. Then, without warning, the strange and terrible Adventure—the only real Adventure she'd ever had—had happened, scarring her life ever after.

She had been so restless in those faraway spring days. Nearly eighteen, a virgin still—technically, at least—and looking toward a future with Hale predictably possessing the texture and flavor of their long-established relationship. So, perhaps, it had happened because of Hale's tender solicitude for her virginity.

Every night he would draw back ostentatiously from their heavy petting, saying in theatrical agony: "Of course, we can *do* it, because we're getting married in June. But . . . I just won't let myself. You must have your wedding night, like any decent girl."

He was getting *his,* all right, from her stroking hand —every time he wanted it. But, afterward, she went to her lonely bed aching from the denial of her own strong hungers. She was ready for him to *do* it, for God's sake, and the fool didn't know it. He would have been shocked if she had told him.

Whether for that reason—or another, more complicated, motive—an impulsive perversity had tempted her to beg Billy-Bob Radley, the day he had first showed it off so proudly in front of their drugstore hangout, for a ride in his graduation-gift convertible. She had just happened to be there, for once, without good old Hale in attendance.

"Sure, hop in," Billy-Bob said readily.

Ignoring the scandalized glares of her envious girl friends, she hopped in. Billy-Bob headed out of town at high speed, leaning back and steering with one hand, with great savoir faire, as he bragged about the technical excellences of his new wheels. Billy-Bob, the center on the football team, was a great hulk of hairy strength, as mature as a grown man. He was, along with all the others on the first string, one of Hale's best friends.

Terrified now by her temerity, she sat silent and subdued. Only when they were far out of town, speeding along a country road, did she speak tentatively: "Don't you think we ought to turn around, Billy-Bob? Everybody will be wondering where we've gone."

His response was to increase the speed of the car. Knowing Billy-Bob's whispered reputation among the senior girls—and wasn't that why she had asked him for the ride?—she began to be truly afraid. When he slowed, abruptly, to take a turn-off road into a stand of trees surrounding two picnic tables, she found herself holding on to the door with one clenched fist to keep from swaying against his great bulk.

He bumped the car to a halt beyond the concrete tables. He turned to her. He said, "OK, babe. Lay it down there on them seat covers so I can get at it."

"What . . . what are you talking about?"

He grinned. "*You* know what I'm talking about. Old Hale, he's been bragging about what a great fuck you are. And Old Billy-Bob has been standing around just drooling, watching you flaunt your horny cunt at me all year long. Now my time has come!"

The revelation of Hale's braggart ways made her cringe inside. "Well, you can think whatever you want to think!" she flared indignantly. Her voice slowed into coldness. "You can also take me back to town this very minute."

He leaned across the seat to lay the weight of his thick arm across her chest. With the other hand, he reached with ruthless precision under her dress and snatched out the bottom of her underpants. The sudden violence made her breathless. Frantically, she tried to squirm away, but there was no struggling against that dead weight of arm. His other hand gripped her nest so hard it hurt, two fingers working deep inside.

"Just hold on, now," he said grimly. "In just about a minute, you're gonna be letting me know how much you love to be finger-fucked."

Helpless, she submitted. When finally he eased up, he sniffed lewdly at his fingers, saying with a grin, "You smell

35

like you're just about ready. So spread it, baby, because, ready or not, old Billy-Bob is coming in."

She sat up away from him, feeling herself sweaty and crumpled and angry. Gasping, "I'm getting out of here," she snatched at the door handle. As she fled from the car, Billy-Bob bailed out over the door on the other side with astonishing speed and agility for such a big man. Before she had run more than ten feet, he had caught her.

Whirling her about, he picked her up bodily and marched into the woods. Cradled in his overpowering arms, she was again helpless.

"Billy-Bob," she said warningly. Behind the words, she was thinking, I'm going to get raped, and it's my own fault. Because I *wanted* it, something inside me decided Billy-Bob, not Hale, would be the first. He's right, I *have* been alert to him for a long time now in all his great hairy strength, so much more of a man than Hale even if Hale *is* a fullback and gets to run with the ball.

Unceremoniously he dumped her on the ground and placed a sneakered foot on her belly to hold her down. He grinned. "Now, pretty thing, I'm gonna show you what you're gonna get."

He unzipped his fly, pulled out his bird. She stared. It was twice as thick, much longer, than Hale's sweet bird in her coyly ministering hand. It stood in great erection, the head a purplish red, jerking tautly against his belly.

"How *about* that, baby?" Billy-Bob bragged. "I've *viewed* that little old wienie Old Hale calls a cock. Now you gonna know what a *man* feels like."

She bit down hard on her lip, averting her eyes. Her voice stammered. "I don't care *what* Hale says. We've never done it, I . . . *I've* never done it."

He stared. "You mean, he's been *lying* all this time? Why, that dirty dawg! He's had the whole team staggering around with the stone ache, telling about how you just fuck a fellow right up the wall."

Hope lived in her. "He's lying," she said firmly. "In fact, Hale has *insisted* on waiting until our wedding night. Now, let me up from here and take me home."

A new idea glowed in his eyes as he whispered terrifying words. "Cherry time. Oh, boy, sweet cherry time."

"Billy-Bob. I always thought you were a gentleman." She hated the wheedling tone of her voice.

He grinned more broadly still. "Two things I ain't no gentleman about, virgin woman. That's football and that's fucking."

He began to unbutton his short-sleeved shirt, exposing the black hair matted in curls on his chest. When he unbelted his pants, dropping them with his jockey shorts and stepping out of them, she saw that the pelt grew thickly down across his belly, merging with the curly mass of hair heavy in his groin. Staring down at her, vaingloriously he rippled his muscles, a great hairy beast out of childhood nightmares come to take her, devour her, use her up.

"Now, you want to slide out of them clothes, or do you want me to *tear* 'em off?"

He would do it. Thinking how it would look, returning to civilization with her clothing torn and dirtied, she reluctantly sat up to obey his bidding.

He watched avidly as she made herself naked. "Cherry time," he whispered again. "You don't know how lucky you are, baby. I'm gonna ruin you for any other man the rest of your life, sweet thing, because I'm an animal when it comes to fucking. Just pure *animal*."

She shuddered all over again, remembering out of her secret watching how he plunged out at the snap of the ball, all that great hairy strength scattering the opposing linemen like tenpins. He was a ruthless man. And by now she knew it was going to happen to her; that terrible, hairy strength was going to explode inside her body.

"Please, Billy-Bob," she whimpered. "Please."

He leaned over to grip shoulders brutally and push her down. "Next thing you know, you'll be *begging* me for it," he said. "Get ready, now. For here comes old Billy-Bob."

In a last hopeless surge of defiance, she crossed her legs, as her mother had taught her to do in an emergency. Billy-Bob simply placed a hand on each thigh and spread her. Then, kneeling between her trembling legs, he poked that huge bird against her cringing nest, grunting as he lay down on her.

She could feel it shoving hard at the door of her body. Then, before she could catch her breath, it was like a knife in her flesh, so huge and hurting that she made a small scream as it broke through. Billy-Bob grinned lustfully, his heavy loins slamming against her body as he began to come. She screamed inwardly, *Don't make a baby in me, Billy-Bob, don't make a baby!* And, as suddenly as he had started, he lay finished, his inert weight smothering her.

She believed it was over. As quickly, she realized in renewed horror that Billy-Bob was only beginning. He rolled over to lie beside her on the rough ground, gripping her with one arm against another attempt to escape as he forced her to caress his bird.

Soon, too soon, it had risen anew into a hard strength, and again he was upon her. His fierce bird thrust deeply again and again, and he *was* an animal, a great, hairy, insatiable animal fucking and fucking and fucking her until, without warning, she began going wild. Clawing at his gross body with clutching hands, her head strained back, she began making strange and terrible sounds of her own as an awful ecstasy ripped heedless through her tortured flesh.

Chuckling and grinning, Billy-Bob eased off deliberately to stroke and toy with her gasping passion, chortling after each helpless response of her body, "Love it, don't you, baby? Didn't I *tell* you you'd love it?"

Tiring finally of the game, he concentrated on achieving a final ejaculation, and at last she could sit up. She hid her face in her arms, feeling herself bedraggled and besmeared with his come, his dirt, his sweat, and cried her heart out in utter misery.

His voice was uneasy. "Aw, now, come on, baby. You know you liked it. I just had to get you over the hump, that's all. But then you loved it, didn't you? Any real woman would."

She glared at him. "Yes. I just loved it, and I hate you for it," she said bitterly. "When I get home, I'm going to have you arrested for rape."

His gaze became stony. "You got into my new car, didn't you? Didn't nobody have to *make* you. So who's gonna believe any little tale you decide to tell?"

He was right, and she knew it. Wearily she got to her feet and stooped after her clothing. She got dressed, picking up last of all the underpants with the bottom ripped out. She gazed at them in disgust, threw them away.

Without looking at Billy-Bob, she said, "Are you going to take me back to town, or do I have to walk?"

"Sure," he said heartily. "Come on, I'll take you back."

"Not to the drugstore," she said, beginning to weep again with the thought. "They'll look at us just once, and they'll *know*."

"Get in," he said generously. "I'll drive you straight home."

But then, that night, when she refused to come out of her room to greet Hale, she had let the cat out of the bag anyway. Because of course Hale knew something had happened and, next day at school, he confronted her. She told him, out of a congealed remoteness, that she had gone riding yesterday in Billy-Bob's new car, and she wasn't sure anymore whether she wanted to marry him in June. Or ever.

Hale was away from her for two interminable weeks. She lived through the dreary days convinced that her body was making a baby out of the mass of come Billy-Bob had heedlessly ejaculated into her nest; somehow she had got the notion that a great quantity of semen was more likely to start a baby than a single orgasm. At last the day came when she knew, with a heartfelt sigh of relief, that she had escaped that peril.

The next night, Hale came to the house, insisting on seeing her. Sitting in the front-porch swing, with space ostentatiously between them, he told her that, in spite of Billy-Bob, he meant to marry her.

When at last she had consented, and they had kissed, he

had said soberly, manfully: "After all, it's too late in life to start with another sweetheart, isn't it?"

Hale was halfway through now; two minutes gone, two minutes to go. His steady little bird, despite all remembering, felt good in her warming nest. Hale was a good man, a gentle man; in their years together, he had not spoken of Billy-Bob—though on their wedding night he had been utterly impotent—and so she moved under him and with him, nurturing a wifely tenderness.

Then, involuntarily, she thought: That man today, he was hairy, too. Not as hairy as Billy-Bob, not that kind of a brute, but . . .

But suppose she *did* meet him, Next Thursday, and he laid her down half against her will, as Billy-Bob had done? Would it drive her crazy, as Billy-Bob had driven her crazy, making her thrash helplessly from one crescendo of orgasm to the next . . . ?

Her hands clutched at Hale as, in a quick surge, she began to come before he was ready to come, bucking under him, holding on, so that Hale paused, startled. With enthusiasm, he began again, he was coming with her, and it was great, wonderful, it was simply marvelous that at this moment a bird was in her nest, to come with her coming.

Hale sprawled away, gasping, "Hey, what was *that* all about?" She soothed him with a stroking hand, with sweet words saying how good he was, until, satisfied in mind as in body, he subsided into completion.

Long after Hale was peacefully snoring, she lay with eyes open upon darkness. She knew that, when Next Thursday came, she would be with the man she had met today.

The Two:

He was not looking for her today because, last Thursday, he had been so greatly baffled in his expectation. When he saw the station wagon, far down the deserted road, he did not believe he saw it, because her arrival at the rendezvous did not fit with the firm set of his mind against a further disappointment.

Only when she stopped the car beside him did he cease pedaling. Alighting, he kicked down the stand and carefully balanced the bike against it.

"Well, hello," he said through the open window.

"I've got ice cream among the groceries, I can't stay long," she said breathlessly, not looking at him. She added unnecessarily, "Butter pecan, it's Hale's favorite."

He hesitated, unsure whether to get in. She reached over to unlock the door in invitation.

"I looked for you last week," he said accusingly. "I wasn't looking for you today, I figured you'd decided . . ."

He brought the smell of male sweat into the car, edging the air-conditioned air. She could not tell him that she had not been here last Thursday because she had been having her period.

"I told you. I wasn't sure I'd come," she said defensively.

Still without looking at him, both hands on the steering wheel, she gazed down the road as though still driving. She expected him to touch her now, kiss her, come at her in one way or another. Perhaps the sure reach of a hand between her legs, up under the loose skirt . . . and he would know, then, that she was naked to him. Naked. And wet. And vulnerable. It did not make any difference that all day long, even while shopping in the grocery store, she had continued to assure herself she would only *be* there, only see him once more; surely it was unthinkable to make love in broad daylight on the side of an occasionally traveled road.

He sensed how wrong it would be to attempt a kiss; she

remained too remote and unapproachable. Placing both hands firmly on his naked thighs, he braced his arms as though they might disobey.

"I'm not sure I want to get into this, myself, to tell you the truth." He tried a small laugh that didn't work too well. "I never have, you know."

She turned her head to stare at him. A fierceness throbbed in her voice. "Don't start out lying to me. Don't *ever* lie to me. *Please.*"

"*I'm not lying,*" he said in a tone that made her believe it.

She was still watching him. Now her eyes were frightened. "What are we doing here, anyway?" she asked desperately. "You're obviously a happily married man, I'm reasonably happy in *my* marriage. We've both got everything to lose and nothing to gain by a quick romp on the side of the road."

"Making up our minds, I guess," he said thoughtfully. "You've got to make up your mind, I've got to make up mine."

She looked away. A quiet despair in her tone now. "I've never made love in an automobile, not once, even if this *is* the age of the automobile."

"It doesn't have to be on the side of the road like this," he said carefully. "I've got a cabin up on a lake, no more than an hour's drive . . ."

She could not tolerate the idea of *planning.* Yet, if it were to become an Adventure, it would have to be planned, wouldn't it? The Adventures of her mind always happened by happy accident; her mind was incredibly inventive in devising new ways of meeting the men of her daydreams. She was not emotionally prepared for the necessity of practical advance planning.

She was looking at him again. "We don't even *know* each other," she said, still in despair. "I have no idea what kind of man you are. For all I know, you do this all the time, you're practiced in all the moves, a step ahead of me all the way."

He had no answers for that breathless series of statements. He could only say, as helplessly as she, "You know me better than that. Else, you wouldn't be here."

"But I don't," she said. "I *don't.*" She stopped. Her hand reached toward him, trembling, to touch his face. The first voluntary move she had made, it startled him so that he jerked away.

Hurt flooded into her eyes. She said unhappily, "You haven't even offered to kiss me."

He kissed her, twisting in the seat as clumsily as a boy. Her lips were hard-edged, unyielding. He placed a hand against her rib cage, pulling her toward him.

Her body resisted. "There's a car coming."

He looked. Far down the road, a car sped rapidly toward them.

Her voice was fateful. "What if it's someone who knows me?"

It sped past; the driver's head turned briefly to stare at their guilty faces; then he was gone. The swift passage had shattered something that, like a crocus bud tentative in the spring, had started growing between them, jarring them out of the dream of lust they had been weaving. He knew, with a fateful certainty, that he would not have her today. The deprivation put an ache into his groin.

She grieved also for the loss of what had been near enough to taste its sweetness. If the car had not passed, he would have touched her. She could then have put her hand down there, felt that strong bird . . . The shorts were white today, the only blueness a stripe on each hip.

"Why is it that we've never met before?" she said in a harried voice. "Both born and raised here, went to school here, surely we know many of the same people. There should have been a party somewhere, sometime, where we'd have seen each other."

"Maybe we weren't meant to meet until now. Maybe neither one of us was ready."

He felt that way about it, somehow, as though every step toward love had been worked out in advance. At the same time, he realized that he was coming on too seriously, making far too much weight out of the affair.

Not at all the right approach, he told himself dismally. What had she said? *A quick romp by the side of the road.* That's all she wanted, obviously; so surely it was not the first time she had indulged a wayward lust.

But . . . did he seriously intend anything more than that same quick romp? He was first in line to become president of the bank if the Old Man ever decided to retire. He knew full well that banking, even in these modern times, was a stuffy institution. Any hint of scandal . . . and there was, after all, Eleanor to be considered, not to mention the boys, only twelve, most of their education yet to be financed.

As though she had been reading the thoughts flitting through his head, she faced him, a certain resolution in her features.

"So what do we do, exactly? We meet here, then we go to your cabin an hour away? When we get there, we take off our clothes and we"—her voice faltered—"we *fuck*?" Saying the word was an obvious effort. "That's it?"

She had laid it out in plain words as much for herself as for him. Deep inside she was trembling, and she was wet again. She had never said the word "fuck" out loud to a man. Not even Hale.

"I guess that's how it is," he said quietly. "If it *is* at all."

His honesty somehow reassured her fears. "I do want you," she whispered. "I don't know why. But I do."

She expected him to protest his own intense desire, then, like any man, use the admission as a gateway to her body. Somewhat to her disappointment, he made no effort to take advantage.

She said rapidly, "I've known only one other man, besides my husband; him only once, and not because I wanted it. I just got myself into a situation where . . ."

She stopped. She began again. "So why, *now*, just because I bumped you off your bicycle a couple of weeks ago . . . ?"

"I don't know," he said.

She touched his face again, her hand cupping his chin, turning his head to make him look directly into her eyes.

44

Strange that she could touch him, when he found it impossible to touch her.

"But . . . will it be *good* enough?" she asked intensely. "Will we do it once, and let that be enough? Or will it go on and on, forever, so that you are my life, and I am your life?"

"I don't know," he said.

She took her hand away. "Why did you meet me if you don't know?" she said bitterly. "If you weren't ready to seduce me . . . You want me to do it all, don't you? Then, if it goes bad, it's my fault. You won't have to feel the least bit of guilt. About me, *or* your wife."

He stirred, bracing himself against the sudden attack. "It's not like that," he protested. "It's just . . . it's just that I don't intend to wrestle you for it." His hand found her arm, gripped it. "We're not a couple of kids, you know, groping each other in a parked automobile. We're *adults*, for God's sake."

Without warning—as she had half-expected all along —his hand had moved to her leg, was sliding up, sliding up, finding bare flesh as her body opened to him. She heard the faint gasp when he discovered her ultimate nakedness.

He trembled violently as though, like a boy, he had never touched a woman. She moved against him as he put two fingers into her; she sighed a deep sigh and reached hungrily for his crotch.

At last she had grasped her body's desire. Though his damned shorts were too tight to get under, she could feel the rigid warmth of his bird through the thin cloth. When she massaged it feverishly, to her delight the head burgeoned forth from under the edge, and she was touching it.

Gripping each other, they were breathing hard. They began to kiss, their mouths as violent as their hands upon each other. In a reckless rush of feeling, they had yielded themselves totally to the passion tiding up over their reasonable conversation.

He felt her starting a quick, fierce orgasm. Though he did not want to come yet—he meant, by God, to lay her down and fuck her madly on this cramped front seat of the

45

station wagon—he couldn't help coming. Groaning in frustration, he felt the orgasm escape his attempt at control. Finished as suddenly as they had started, they lay crumpled against each other, still helplessly touching because they were both so greatly dissatisfied with the disheveled incompletion. She sat up abruptly, gasping, "Oh, my God! Here comes another car."

He straightened, in a panic equal to her own. This driver stared also, curiosity plain on his face; he began to slow down, as though to inquire if help were needed. However, to their enormous relief, he speeded up again and continued onward.

Her voice was shaky. "I can't believe I'm doing this."

"Like two crazy kids," he confirmed.

She looked him straight in the face. Then, bravely, she gazed at his crotch. The shorts were damp with his come. The cock, thick and long even now, lolled brazenly in her view.

Her face was tragic. "It's here, isn't it? Whether we want it or not. Nothing we can do about it. Because, whether we make love or don't make love, it won't go away."

He nodded in assent, feeling the weight of her pronouncement. Underneath, he was thinking: Why are we so grim about it? Shouldn't we be *happy,* for God's sake? Nobody's *driving* us into each other's arms.

She sat quite still. Her voice did not tremble. "I am going to be unfaithful to my husband. I've just got *through* being unfaithful. Like you've just been unfaithful to your wife."

He had to admit her honesty. "It's true." But he added, "It's what we wanted, isn't it? Both of us. As much as we've ever wanted anything."

"Yes. I kept telling myself I would only see you, talk to you, explain how I couldn't . . ." She paused. Then she said, "But I didn't put on underpants today, either."

He leaned to kiss her. "You are a lovely woman." His voice was tender. "As beautiful and honest inside as you're beautiful and honest outside."

"You wouldn't believe the world I've lived in, inside my head, all these years I've been married to Hale," she said in a low voice. "Erotic daydreams, totally shameless, real and romantic at the same time." She shuddered slightly. "The acts I've performed, all in my head, *everything*. And everything done to *me*."

"The lovely girls I've had," he said in equal confession. "Thousands of them, every one different."

"I never believed it could lead to this." She shook her head. "Meeting as we did, an absolute accident, was right out of a daydream. Except you didn't *take* me, as, in my mind, you would have taken me. As in my mind, my body, I *wanted* you to take me."

She breathed again. "But now it's *real*. Too real. There's no way it can be that you've never touched me. That I've never touched you."

"No going back." He was watching her, almost hoping for her assent to the cautious suggestion. "Of course, going on can mean stopping, too. *Not* going on."

"But it's not going to be like that, is it? You're going to fuck me, I'm going to fuck you, and . . ." She stopped. She said in a thoughtful voice, "That's funny. I don't flinch from saying 'fuck' to you, when I've never used that word in my life. But that's what you and I are all about, isn't it? Fucking."

"Yes," he said, adding in a spate of words, "I like it that way. It's the only way it can be."

She smiled, a brilliant smile, and for the first time she looked happy. "All right," she said. "So we fuck." She stretched her body, suddenly languorous. "You know, it's wonderful to just feel it, just say it. *We're going to fuck*."

"What a woman you are," he whispered. His voice deepened in urgency. "There's still time. It's only an hour to the lake. We'll have to hurry, but . . ."

She shook her head. "I've got to get Hale's ice cream into the freezer." She laughed weakly. "It's probably melted by now."

"But . . ."

"No." Her voice was firm. "If we're going to do it, let's do it right. Have time, time enough to . . . " Her breath caught as she looked at him. She looked swiftly away.

47

He put his hand between her legs, trusting to persuade her flesh against her more prudent will. But she fended him off, saying in that breathless tone which warmed his groin so deeply, "Don't start me again. If you start me again, I'll . . ."

He was bereft. "But . . . it's *forever* until Next Thursday."

She smiled as though at an importunate boy. "It'll be here when it's ready to be here."

"Wait a minute," he said quickly. "Tuesday, Eleanor —my wife—will be away overnight for a duplicate-bridge tournament. I'll find an excuse to take off from the bank Tuesday afternoon . . ."

Her voice interposed. "Listen. I'm not going to disrupt your life, you're not going to disrupt mine. One little piece of time—Thursday afternoons—belongs to us. Stealing any other time would be terribly wrong."

He yielded grudgingly. "All right. If that's how it has to be."

Her hand caressed his cheek with a tender fondness. "That's how it *is*." Her tone turned grave. "That's how it must always be. However long it . . ." Her voice faltered. "However long it lasts."

"Don't talk about that. Don't even *think* about it."

They were in each other's arms again, kissing. Tenderly this time, not passionately, each with a sweet acceptance of the other's needs and limitations, their separate burdens of duty and caution and responsibility.

Finally, with reluctance, she disengaged. "I must go now. But . . ." Her eyes were direct and candid, though her mouth trembled with the vow. "I promise: I will be here Thursday. I will go with you to your cabin on the lake."

The vow satisfied him. "Thursday it is," he said. He got out, held the bicycle upright to kick up the stand. He turned to see her one last time through the windshield.

Putting her head out the window, she said cheerfully, "You look a mess."

Ruefully he glanced down at the front of his shorts. She laughed, suddenly gleeful. "And so am I."

With a startling roar of the overpowerful motor, she was gone, the wheels spinning as she scratched out onto the blacktop. He mounted his bike and began pedaling slowly toward home. In a few minutes, he heard her coming back. He put one foot down to steady himself, hoping against hope that she would stop to declare that she was ready to fuck him right now. But she only waved as she went by, a quick flicker of a vanishing hand.

The Woman:

In the following days, she saw herself as two different people.

She first realized it when Nancy and Pam called from camp half an hour after she was safely home. Beneath their happy chatter about prizes and projects, the *neat* swimming instructor they had this year, she could feel in herself the great contrast between the motherly thing she was doing now, the womanly thing she had done this afternoon.

Murmuring appropriate responses to their happy enthusiasm, she wondered how—if somehow they knew—the knowledge of her recent activities would strike at them. What *would* they think, feel, if she should tell them that this afternoon her hand had held a strange man's bird, had stroked that beautiful bird into a great coming that had pumped wetly over her cupped fist?

But of course children don't believe love-making, even between parents, is really possible where their mother is concerned. She herself, at the age of the Gold Dust Twins, had possessed a theoretical knowledge of sexual intercourse. But she had found it quite impossible to visualize her mother copulating with her father. The bedroom of her parents had been as sacrosanct as the bedroom she shared with Hale.

Facing her complacent husband across the dinner table, she experienced the division in herself more strongly still. Comfortable with his familiar presence, watching him eat with his usual slow enjoyment, she was split into two entirely different females.

With the sole exception of her fantasy life, she had never guarded secrets from Hale. The sexual daydreams, after all, had existed before the wedding, a compartment of her life private from all other human beings. Except, now, she had told *him*, which meant, didn't it, that *he* was closer to her than anyone had ever been.

She remembered how Billy-Bob had gleefully told her how Hale had bragged of fucking her. So Hale—at least as an adolescent—had also owned a private fantasy life, in which he was the proud conqueror and possessor of her flesh. She could understand, and so forgive, that in his male world of high-school athletics he was ashamed to confess to virginity.

I suppose everyone, really, keeps a satisfying sex life warm and secret in her thoughts, she reflected in a flash of clarity. Tacitly, she had always believed she had invented fantasy sex. Just as, an adolescent, she had been guiltily convinced she was the only girl who had ever masturbated.

This, now; *this* was different. *This* was real. Today, for the first time since Billy-Bob, she had been touched by a man other than Hale. It made a fundamental difference in her world, as in herself.

Sure, she thought deeply behind the casual dinner-table conversation, it's supposed to be a new world, here in the 1980s. For ten or fifteen years now, sex of all varieties has emerged triumphantly from the closet. People live together without being married; there are open marriages in which both partners fuck anybody they want to fuck. Girls only thirteen, fourteen years old come up pregnant, a real problem in the schools—soon now, too soon, we'll have to start worrying about the Gold Dust Twins—but somehow or other none of this has touched my own life.

I have dwelled, she reflected, in an insulated and comfortable—admit it, rather boring—existence, wrapped in safe cocoons of sufficient money and sufficient status, of a marriage totally safe and totally predictable.

She realized, with a panicking of her heart, the danger she had, this afternoon, accepted into the established solar system of her life. Lust, like a blazing comet hurtling in from the cold reaches of outer space in her soul, had swept devastatingly across her serene skies, foreboding who knew what terrible disasters and misfortunes. Not only exposure, scandal . . . a profound alteration of herself into a woman she had never been.

"Good dinner," Hale said, putting down his dessert

spoon with a sigh of satisfaction. "I'm glad you remembered butter pecan is my favorite ice cream." As though she ever forgot; it was only that the twins so often demanded exotic flavors.

With Hale safely ensconced at his card table, she busied herself clearing the table. As she rinsed the dishes and loaded the dishwasher, she told herself firmly: So this is how it's going to be now. I'll just have to learn how to handle it.

There was in her no wish to deny the promise of Next Thursday she had made to her lover. Her *lover*. Her body flushed warmly with the meaning of those words. *After twenty years of faithful marriage, she had a lover*.

It was surely fated. Something within her had been waiting for a secret lover, the erotic daydreams only a rehearsal of real events of the flesh to arrive upon the stage of her being. Like the time she had begged Billy-Bob Radley to take her for a ride in his brand-new convertible; something in her had *known* that she was seeking a surrender of her virginity to a man other than dull, reliable old Hale. It was, she had understood even as it was happening, a last-minute rebellion against life with Hale as it would surely be lived.

Today, then? Was it also a rebellion against her life as it had unfolded through twenty years?

She examined the idea. She did not want it to be merely a mindless rebellion, as Billy-Bob had been. She yearned for it to change her, profoundly and forever. Though she had no inkling what that change would entail.

Yet—could she accept a sea change in her self that would force a choice between the life she knew and a life she could not even visualize? She didn't think so—and right now, so early in the Adventure, when she had not yet experienced that wonderful new bird in her nest, she didn't want to think about it.

So, then. What, exactly, was it?

Quite simply, what she had told *him* in the beginning. A romp in the hay. Self-indulgence of a deep and private need, belonging far more to the realm of her fantasies than to the solar system of her life.

She told herself happily: I will act out my lifelong fantasy of total sexual involvement with a beautiful stranger. Suddenly liberated, she gloried in her new self . . . *both* of her selves. They were, after all, twin parts of the woman she had always been. There was now room in her life for the secret wanton, as for the wife and mother.

She entered the living room quietly, found a paperback novel she hadn't read, sat down with it. Over its opened pages she studied Hale, absorbed in his nightly agenda of paper work. I have now started to build a separate life, she thought, and you, dear Hale, will never know.

It will be necessary to plan a block of time each Thursday afternoon to be with my lover, she reminded herself. Our secret time, out of each of our lives. But then, all through my years with Hale, I have been in training for such a double life.

She wondered, suddenly, if Hale held secrets from her. She had never considered that disturbing possibility. Hale was such an *open* person. But what if—out of town, maybe at a bar association convention—he had indulged in the experience of another woman? A casual encounter in a bar, perhaps leading to a one-night stand?

Since she had now betrayed him, at least in desire and intent, she generously hoped it *had* happened. Yet, watching Hale from across the room, she found it impossible to believe. In the ninth grade, he had chosen her for the woman of his life. He had not allowed even the crisis of Billy-Bob Radley to turn him aside from that certain path.

Except that, on their wedding night, he had been impotent. Except that, on their wedding night, he had cried.

Hale glanced up, an absent-minded smile on his face. Amazing, how often people will become subliminally aware that someone is thinking deeply about them.

She closed her book and stood up, stretching. "I don't know about you, but I'm going to bed."

"A tiring day?"

"Yes," she said. "All that grocery shopping . . . everything."

He gestured toward the scatter of papers. "Be in soon. Got to finish this stuff first, though, for court tomorrow. It's the Halloran case, finally coming to trial."

Going into the bedroom, she panicked inwardly. What if, tonight of all nights, he came to her with bottom bare, seeking sex?

In her new double life, she realized, she would be compelled to yield her body to both husband and lover. Perhaps, at times, within the span of the same day.

But not tonight, she prayed. Not until I have had *his* pretty bird hard and hot inside my warm nest.

The Man:

In the following days, he saw himself as two different people.

It scared the hell out of him.

At dinner that night, listening to Eleanor detail card by card how her partner had managed to blow a sure-fire grand slam, he thought: What the *hell* do I think I'm doing?

Not only Eleanor, the boys, the house; it was the bank, his job, his career. He had carried it out successfully so far; though starting in a teller's case, for God's sake, even with his Harvard MBA, because it was the Old Man's basic tenet that every employee must begin by dealing with the dime-and-dollar customer. There had been the bad years, after Eleanor had married him, when his cohorts and underlings had cynically believed that he had married the boss's daughter to further his career. He had survived his first year as credit manager, when the bad-loan statistics had given him a terrible black eye, though it had been as much the fault of the economy as of his decisions.

To risk the work of a lifetime for the sake of a strange piece of ass!

If that was all he wanted, it would be easy enough to arrange a trip, get laid safely out of town. If he didn't want to risk cruising bars, five hundred dollars, for God's sake, would buy the greatest call girl in the world.

An episode, at any rate, safely compartmented from his life, not worth a minute's worth of worry. He knew from his bachelor days how easy it was to get your ashes hauled. The world, he told himself, is full of panting girls ready for a handsome man with a great body, even if he does show a touch of gray in his hair.

He remembered the startlingly efficient new secretary with the beautiful legs who had let him know quite openly that she was available. Out of sheer self-defense, he had been forced to fire her ass.

He wondered why his mind was phrasing these thoughts so crudely. It was not the natural set of his mind to think of women in such terms. He *liked* women, he even believed in women's lib, for God's sake.

If the Old Man ever made up his mind to retire, all he'd need would be ten years as president of the bank. Retire himself then, build The Aerie up there on the lake. Of course, he wouldn't be able, actually, to live the wild life of his daydreams. But certainly, by unselfishly allowing Eleanor to stay in town most of the time for her bridge, he'd earn a great deal of solitude. With the career no longer at stake, it might even be possible to run in a girl friend or two, if he were discreet about it.

He'd be no more than fifty-five by then; young enough by any standard. And still, he knew, in great physical condition, looking years younger, because he'd always be careful to keep up the schedule of exercises.

Sitting at the dinner table, not listening to Eleanor, he couldn't believe himself this afternoon. In broad open daylight, on the front seat of that station wagon, wrestling with each other like a couple of sweaty teen-agers. He was known by hundreds, even thousands, of people in this town; he was a *public person*, for God's sake, and it could have been *anybody* driving by. Boy, wouldn't they love to scatter the story, too!

If she had only allowed him, he'd have shucked off naked and fucked her regardless of circumstance or consequence. Talk about letting your goddamned cock run your life!

Watching Eleanor as she indignantly related her woeful tale of how badly her partner had played today, he found it incredible that she could not see it in him. Eleanor, from the beginning, had known him, understood him, better than anyone. So why, now, could she not recognize instinctively that today he had fondled another woman's pussy, had owned an aching hard-on only half-assuaged by the orgasm *she* had given him with her rapid hand.

God, when he had reached his hand up under her dress! Naked and ready, she had opened her legs, she had reached for him with a greedy hand. How she must have wanted to touch his cock, *feel* it. The very first day, she had stared hard at his crotch, wanting it so badly it was a wonder she hadn't gone down on him then and there.

He had always heard—it was even stated in books on the psychology of the female—that women did not visualize the act of sex as graphically as a man did. Specifically, it was asserted that the size of a man's cock meant nothing to a woman, emotionally or physically.

He had never believed it. Those romantic yearnings females were supposed to have instead, he was firmly convinced, were a myth created by the women themselves. It was a part of the mystery women collectively conspired to maintain against the males of the species. How could a woman, when she visualized being fucked, not yearn for a strong cock, hard and driving?

His mind reverted to *her*. She had warned him against lying; when, all the time, *she* was lying, with that silly claim it was new to her, too. So open and honest in her lusts—he *liked* that in her—he'd bet large money she'd already had a dozen lovers. That poor husband of hers, she probably kept him fat, dumb, happy . . . and blind.

And poor Eleanor? He shied away from that thought.

Eleanor, rising briskly from the table, asked if he would put out the garbage after she'd cleaned up the kitchen. She knew, of course, that he would; she always asked anyway. The garbage out, he went into the garage, flicking on the light switch beside the door. Deliberately he made himself naked before the broad sweep of glass.

He put congratulatory hands on his tool, thinking, Yes, she *wanted* that old cock, she *loved* it. It would be marvelous, he knew already, to fuck that sweet pussy. But . . . would it be worth it? Just once, and then no more? he wondered. After all, he'd gone this far.

Yet, standing before the weight-lifting mirror, looking at his naked body with the warm memories of the afternoon stirring in his blood, he believed that Next Thursday he would not meet her. He would not take her to the cabin. He would not fuck her.

It was stupid.

To follow blindly his blind cock, he would have to deny the man he had become: Bank Vice-President, Husband, Father. Love was not—*could* not be—the important thing in a man's life as it was, always, to a woman. That, he felt sincerely, was the basic difference between male and female. He was, if nothing else, a *man*. He was, if nothing else, a rising young banker, a faithful and devoted husband.

She had said this afternoon that, by the mere touching of each other, the unconsummated lust they had shared, they had already committed adultery. No. Adultery would be when he put his cock into her cunt, when he fucked her and fucked her and fucked her until she was coming and, pronged deeper into her than any man had ever been, he was coming, too.

His cock had got hard with the heated thoughts. Unconsciously, his hand was slowly stroking as he stood with tensely braced legs. Years since he had masturbated; sternly he took away the tempting hand. He thought of Eleanor, in bed by now, probably half asleep. Eleanor would do him. She always did, whenever he asked.

It wouldn't be fair, though, to bring to Eleanor the leavings of lust for another woman. Not once had he broken the bargain with Eleanor. This afternoon, with his near approach to a thrust into that beautiful pussy, he had come perilously close. But he had not, he had not—and, now that he had come to his senses, he never would.

Nor would he take this random, roadside lust to his wife. He would wait until Eleanor expected him on Sunday night, in the once-a-week pattern she had established after the twins had been born.

Sunday night, Eleanor turned to him as a matter of course. Her hand touched first his chest, slid down his naked belly, lingered over his limpness. Sensing her surprise that he was not ready, he said apologetically, "You'll have to do me, I guess."

As, with generous eagerness, Eleanor's mouth came on him, he found himself wondering if *she* was making love tonight. He felt sure of it; they seemed unconsciously to ride on the same roller coaster of desire. They had almost surely got their children on the same night of their lives; indeed, it felt strangely as though, those many years ago, his seed had spurted into the wrŏng womb.

If he went to *her* on Thursday, he would be taking the risk of experiencing her with the memory of another man's cock in her flesh . . . for how could he know she had not fucked her husband the night before?

He had never in his life, to his knowledge, fucked a woman still warm from another man's cock. Certainly not since Eleanor had married him; he had been the only man to enter Eleanor, then or since, for she had come virgin to their marriage.

This was, he knew, rank jealousy. How could he possibly be jealous of a woman—nearly a stranger—for having honest sex with her husband? But—he knew in his deepest instincts, as real as if he were a Peeping Tom, that she was fucking at this very moment. Remembering with all his senses the heat of her cunt against his fingers, he thought: She's like that now, greedy for it like she was greedy for *my* cock. By God, he'd have her yet. Just once. Just to show her.

When Eleanor's mouth retreated, the pressure of her hands on his thighs signaling that she wished him on top now, he resisted mutely. Unreasonably, yet stubbornly, he did not want to experience the sensation of Eleanor's soft belly at the very instant he was visualizing how *her* body, slim but strong with passion, would feel when he stretched his own lean-bellied frame full-length upon her.

Eleanor, sighing patiently, straddled herself on top, her bottom absorbing the hard-on her mouth had commanded. This, too, was an occasional and accepted variation of their pattern, Eleanor upright over his loins, her body weight heavy on his flesh as he lay passive under her slowly writhing loins.

As Eleanor fucked him, he concentrated vividly on how he would fuck *her* Next Thursday . . . the hard cock driving into her again and again until she screamed with anguish and ecstasy, hands clawing at his back, surrendered so completely to his rampant cock that she didn't know, anymore, what she was doing.

Even with the prurient vision seductive in his mind, his orgasm was slow in arriving. When at last he did come, however, it was prolonged, with a passive sweetness that fulfilled a long-pent-up need.

After his orgasm, Eleanor segued deftly into the concentrated, wriggling grind that brought her off so separately it seemed as though he, his cock, had nothing to do with it. Still, grateful, he held her for a time in his arms, loving his wife the way a man ought to love his wife, not allowing himself to think again about how he'd show *her*.

Just once. For once would be enough.

The Woman:

Sunday night, when Hale came bottom-naked to bed, she sought desperately for an excuse to deny him. Not because of Hale himself. Habit was strong enough, habit *and* love, she assured herself, to make it easy to yield her flesh.

Because of herself. She was deathly afraid that, like the last time, anticipation of her lover would dwell so strongly in her flesh she would again startle Hale with an unexpected passion. The risk was too great; several times, the day after, she had caught Hale watching her, puzzled speculation in his eyes. In her state of marital sin, she could not afford to arouse his suspicions.

Never having established the capacity of No, a denial now would only arouse more suspicion. Grimly, she told herself, I must be exactly as good for him—and no better —as always.

She set her mind firmly against flinching as she ringed his bird with thumb and forefinger. She did not allow in her awareness the inevitable perception that Hale's little dickie-bird was not nearly so big as *his* bird.

Hale, as usual, was quickly ready. She took him coldly, feeling him small in her empty nest and realizing in fresh despair that, his flesh sensing the cool reception, he was rapidly losing his erection. She forced herself into movement, simulating what she did not feel. Hale, easily satisfied as always, began the steady four-minute humping that inevitably brought him to a satisfactory ejaculation.

She lay with head back, staring at the darkened ceiling, as she held at bay all sense of *him*. Soon enough, however, she realized that, fearful of giving too much, she was not giving enough. I've got to do better, she reminded herself. If I can't make love with my husband because of *him*, it's not going to work. Hale, sweet and loving and believing as he is, does have his sensitivities.

She let *him* in then, carefully, just enough to warm her flesh. Not Next Thursday—she couldn't bear that—but last week; the memory of how his beautiful bird had felt in her hand, the head of it peeping out from under the tight shorts, blindly seeking her warm nest.

Hale, responding to the new warmth, began to come and she could tell, from the way the soft weight of his body collapsed upon her, that it was as good as always for him. Putting both hands on the nape of his neck, she held him, as he liked to be held in the minute after, and felt miserably like a whore.

This misery, she knew now, was the price to be paid for Next Thursday. But now that it *is* paid, she thought like a reasonable woman, there is nothing to keep me from enjoying the reward.

The Two:

He put the bicycle into the station wagon, moving the grocery sacks to do so. Over her shoulder she said with a grin, "No ice cream today."

He kept a withdrawn silence. When he got into the front seat, she looked at him uncertainly. "Hello."

He cleared his throat. "How are you?"

"Fine. Just fine." Then: "You'll have to tell me where we're going."

"Oh, sure, yeah," he said quickly and began to give directions in a blurred, hasty voice. She put the car into gear—she had not stopped the motor—but then, foot on brake pedal, she said bravely, "Look. We don't *have* to do this."

His voice was apologetic. "Yes. We do. It's just that . . . I'm feeling guilty as hell, that's all."

"Join the company," she said shortly. Her mood changed for the better. "This is supposed to be fun 'n' games, isn't it? If it isn't fun 'n' games, what are we here for?"

"I'm just not used to . . . You know."

She snapped, "Do you think *I* am?" Anger now. She couldn't seem to control the rapid pendulum of her feelings.

For the first time today, they looked at each other at the same moment. Their eyes met, clung, darted away. When they returned again, to look deeply, she felt her breath catch short. *Yes. She was going to make love with this man. Soon now. Very soon.*

. Not make love, she told herself. *Fuck.* Fuck this man.

"Straight about three miles, then take a left, right?" she said unnecessarily as she pulled out into the road. Behind them, the bicycle rattled intrusively. On their way now, no turning back. Yet between them dwelled only a remote silence, not yet a warmth of conspiracy, of being at last together in the flesh as in their lustful minds.

She broke the silence. "Have you . . . been thinking of me?"

The answer was abrupt, unwilling. "Yes."

She was so much farther away today, as though he had never touched her. Or ever could. Intimidated, he was dismayingly convinced that, when the time came for performance, he wouldn't be able to perform.

Unable to bear the terrible probability, he leaned forward to put a hand between her legs. Concentrating on the driving, she gave him no response, not even a smile of acknowledgment. As quickly as he had reached, he took his hand away, saying shortly, "Sorry."

Her head turned in protest against his shy assumption of her untouchableness. But now the silence was in her, for she was thinking how impossible it would be to make herself naked before him.

With Hale, *naked* was always under the bed covers. She had never touched Hale within the sight of her eyes. Why it should be so, she did not know. When Hale came to bed without the bottom half of his pajamas, she could certainly, if she so desired, see his erection. Except, Hale never had an erection until she had aroused his bird with ringed thumb and forefinger. And I've got to quit calling it by that silly name, she told herself in astonishing fury.

This man, she knew, would demand a naked woman. He would gaze at her breasts, her crotch; and she knew with dismay that the thigh muscles were not as firm as they used to be.

What if the sight of her naked body turned him off?

She realized, suddenly, that behind the doubtful anticipation of making herself naked for him, she was dwelling on *his* nakedness. *Thinking* of him being naked as she had never envisioned any man . . . except in her greatest fantasies.

Not that the shorts he wore for bicycling left much to the imagination. An excellent body, the muscles smooth and rippling, his step elastic. Only . . . he was so *hairy*. She shivered inside. Being under *him* would be like that time

64

with Billy-Bob, when she had been fucked by an animal of a man.

A long drive, nearly an hour, far too long for the silence lengthening between them. He tried without success to think of a safe topic for conversation. There was only the one. But it was impossible to talk about what they meant to do once they reached the cabin.

He carried not only the guilt for having consented in his soul to betray Eleanor with this woman; there was also the guilt of having thought about *her*, the entire week, in that crude way of thinking. She would never let him touch her if she knew.

He had done it, he knew, only to persuade himself, by holding her cheaply in his esteem, that he could afford to keep the rendezvous. *A quick piece of ass.* God, he was such a bastard! He knew now what they meant when they said a hard prick has no conscience.

He was so absorbed in contemplation of his male unworthiness that the station wagon was a mile beyond the turnoff before he noticed.

"Wait a minute, we've overshot it," he said in agitation. "We'll have to go back."

She wished he wouldn't be so damned apologetic. Like any woman, she had counted on following his male lead, persuaded step by step toward consummation. As a man ought to do with a woman he desires so ardently. It was not going to be like that; she would have to march step by step to her own fate of making herself an unfaithful wife.

The realization stirred a tiny, aggressive anger. As she headed the car onto a side road, stopped, backed out into the highway, she said with asperity, "We don't have hours and hours, you know. I have to be home at a decent time. And so do you, I suppose."

"I'm sorry," he said.

"Oh, quit being so damned sorry all the time," she flared.

She was grateful that he did not answer the outburst. She had no wish to pursue anger; any more than, at this moment, she wished to pursue the female lust that had brought her to this time, this place, with this man.

Because that's all it is, she told herself bluntly. *Lust*. The lust to be fucked, just once again in her life, by a hairy man with a huge, hard, hurting bird. *Cock*, damn it. Huge *cock*. She was tired of how her silly mind dodged so nimbly around the realities of things.

Almost immediately after they had entered the cabin road, it narrowed and began to climb steeply. Small branches brushed against the sides of the car. The ungainly station wagon protested in its steel bones against the bumpiness of the terrain.

"Much farther?" she asked apprehensively after a particularly deep pothole.

"No. In fact, we're here," he said as the station wagon moved into a small clearing.

She turned off the motor and sat looking at the cabin. An old farmhouse, actually, too big for the clearing it sat in. It had once been repainted with a greenish stain to make it blend with the surrounding woods. There was a front porch, with two rocking chairs. A chimney betrayed the presence of a fireplace. A farm family had lived in this house, not very prosperously. Down through the treetops, she could see the glint of a small lake between steep hills.

"But it's a *house*," she said, betraying the disappointment engendered by its devastating difference from her visualization of it as the scene of her first real Adventure.

"Yeah, I moved it up here when I bought the land, a few years ago," he said. "Originally, it was built down in a hollow, sheltered from wind and weather. But I wanted the view."

He was seeing the place with her eyes. Certainly not The Aerie of his dreams. "Didn't stand the moving any too well —too ancient, I guess." He turned to her. "If you'd rather, we can find a motel."

She shook her head. Firmly. "No. I couldn't do that." With an effort, she made herself unlatch the door and step down. She waited until he came around to her side. Clutching his arm, she found the courage to walk up the path into the place where, for the first time, they would make love. *Fuck*, she told herself. *Fuck*.

On the porch she paused, waiting for him to usher her inside. He did not move to do so, only unlocking the door and standing aside.

She mustered a wan smile. "Well, welcome to the old homestead," she said in a forlorn attempt at gaiety.

He followed her into the living room. The furniture was shabby and mismatched: an old sofa, two or three chairs, scarred tables. Obviously, the cabin was furnished with cast-offs.

"Want a drink?"

"No," she said. "I don't care . . ." And then, "Yes. Yes."

Looking relieved, he led the way to the kitchen. The ice tray in the freezer compartment was frosted heavily from long disuse. He took it to the sink to run water over the cubes.

Blended whiskey. She had never liked blended whiskey, but she drank it gratefully. They stood uncertainly in the kitchen, holding their glasses, not looking at each other.

"We're neither one of us much good at this," she said, smiling wanly.

"I guess not."

He had expected everything, once here, to progress smoothly. But, as awkward in his body as in his mind, he had to force himself to move a step closer, putting one arm around her waist to pull her against him. She stood stiffly. At least, she had not refused his embrace. Shifting his glass to the hand behind her back, he put his other hand between her legs, pressing hard against her mount.

"Don't paw me," she said sharply, taking his wrist in a firm grip to separate his hand from her flesh. "I *hate* being pawed."

She's got underpants on today, flashed through his mind. Stubbornly he put the hand again into her fork to verify the impression. She sighed and leaned tightly against his thigh, his palm trapped between their bodies.

"Oh, God," she whispered as though hoping not to be heard. "What are we doing here?"

Her hand found his bird then, discovered that it was not hard, as it had been the first time she had touched it. She

67

could hear their breathing in the quietness of the old house.

She said in the same whisper, "You really haven't ever done this before, have you? No more than I have."

He did not answer. No need to answer; she was closer, she had lifted her mouth for a kiss, he was kissing her. Her lips bloomed under his, warm and seeking. They were both trembling with the desire that was in them.

A very long minute, then she stood away, saying, "Show me the rest of the house."

He knew she meant, *Take me to the place where you're going to fuck me,* so he led her directly to the bedroom.

The sight of the shabby, antique bed with its bare mattress jarred her sensibilities. She stared with wide eyes at its waiting expanse, wanting out of here as fiercely as she had yearned to come.

"I'll find some sheets," he said hastily. While he fumbled in the linen closet in the hallway, she drank greedily from her glass in search of a warming influence.

"I should have come up during the week, gotten things ready," he said as he unfolded the fitted sheet and flapped it over the bed in an unsuccessful effort to flare it neatly flat.

"That's all right," she said with an effort. Putting the glass on the bedside table, she fitted the sheet expertly under the mattress corners.

He was still fumbling helplessly on his side of the bed.

"Get out of the way. I'll do it," she said, coming around to him. She was glad for the busyness. These down-to-earth practicalities of illicit love-making had never intruded upon her fantasies. And we've still got to get out of our clothes before we can be safe and hidden and naked together under the sheet, she thought despairingly.

Top and bottom sheets neatly in place, she made herself sit on the edge of the bed. "Well," she said, a catch in her throat. "Here we are."

He sat down beside her. His arm pressed her backward. As they lay down, he lifted his leg to press between her legs. She endured it for a moment, then sat up, saying,

68

"Don't rumple me, I don't want to go home looking like . . ." Then: "We'll have to get naked, won't we?"

Resolutely she began to undress, trying, without success, to make herself unself-conscious of his watching eyes. Too long since I've done regular exercise, she lamented. He'll see me as too flabby, he won't like my breasts, he . . .

He marveled at the youthfulness of her figure. Eleanor had long since become matronly in the beam, soft in the stomach. This woman showed a slim-lined belly sloping seductively into the shadowed crotch, her ass taut and small. Her skin had a fresh, healthy look, paler than he had expected but flushed with youthful blood.

She stood before him at last, wearing only the panties. Pale blue, he saw, a paler blue than his shorts, shadowed by pubic hair. Looking cold and pinched, she folded her arms across her breasts, hugging herself.

"Well. Are you going to let me get into bed?" she asked plaintively. Her voice trembled with the chill.

He moved out of the way. She dived immediately under the sheet, pulling it hastily over her nakedness.

His turn now. A betraying jerkiness in the movements, he pulled the T-shirt over his head. He unzipped the shorts, hooked his thumbs to push them down. He hesitated, thinking, *Jesus, I don't have a hard-on*. Desperately he willed his cock to rise. It did not, and he could not stand betrayed forever. He pushed down the shorts.

Her gaze shifted, against her will, to the ceiling. The sight of his matted chest, the hair wiry, tinged auburn, had sent a cold shiver through her flesh as she thought of the sensuous tickling on her exposed nipples.

He got in beside her, reaching an arm across to pull her close. He slid the other hand down her belly to the crotch. She still had the panties on. He snugged his hand underneath, found her mount, squeezed it.

The air in the room was hot, moist, with a musty smell. The wooden ceiling was water stained, betraying a sometime leak in the roof. She lay stiffly straight, letting him fondle her. There was not yet a response in her flesh, she felt only cold, *cold*, and she thought miserably, *I'm going to be terrible*.

He was taking off her pants. She lifted her buttocks, allowing them to slip free. At last they were naked together under the sheet. She moved her legs apart and waited for him to come on her.

He didn't move. He was only touching her again, saying with concern, "Are you all right?"

"Yes," she said. "Go ahead and do it."

"But I can tell you're not ready . . ."

"Do it, damn it," she said angrily. "That's what we came for, isn't it? Just *take* me."

That apologetic male voice again. "You'll have to do me first. Will you do me?"

"Do you?" she said, rising up in astonishment. "What do you mean, *do me?*"

"I'm not ready yet, either," he said painfully. "If you'll go down on me . . ."

She stared, puzzlement plain on her face. As a signal of his meaning, he put one hand on the back of her neck, pushing her head down toward his crotch. As she realized in horror what he was asking her to perform, she struggled against the pressure.

"I don't . . . I never . . ." she gasped. Then, in a cold voice: "*I don't do that.*"

The words shriveled his rising lust. What the hell have I got myself into, he thought angrily. It had been the first thing Eleanor had done for him, the *only* thing until they were married. He had always cherished a woman's mouth; he had wanted to feel *her* mouth, sucking, sucking . . .

He sat up. "Listen. I thought you came to fuck."

She flung the answer in his face like a glove. "I thought I came here with a *man*, able and anxious to do his share."

It struck him to the quick. He flung off the sheet, exposing her body. She cringed, curling into herself. Inexplicably, his bird was now rigid in response to denial and frustration. Her eyes widened at the sight of its burgeoning length.

"All right. You came to fuck, you're going to get fucked,"

he said, angrier still, as he put both hands to her shoulders to push her down again.

She surrendered before him, fearful yet tingling. It was *this* she had daydreamed about all week; the hairy man taking her whether or not she wished to be taken, thrusting into her without mercy . . .

He thrust into her without mercy. It hurt, not only because she was so unready, but because his bird was bigger and harder than she was accustomed to receiving. She could only submit limply to the pain of its huge entrance into her cold nest. His body was too heavy on her, too hairy, and it hurt . . . God, so much bigger than Hale's, it was like losing her virginity all over again.

It angered him more than ever that she remained dry, unlubricated. She was not embracing him, but lay with arms outflung, totally surrendered but totally unresponsive. And already he couldn't hold it, he was beginning to come.

She felt him coming. Suddenly her mind pictured this strong, hairy man clamping ruthless hands on her wrists, holding her down while he ejaculated his seed into her. But he did not hold her down, he was only coming in her; and so now she had been fucked by another man, and it was nasty, gross, with no love, no tenderness, not at all as she had dreamed it would be.

The juice spurted angrily, and he felt his cock begin to die. He was miserable with defeat. He had taken her in anger when he had yearned for it to be accomplished in love and in lust. Sprawled on her supine body, he put his face into the slope of her neck, seeking warmth.

"Did you come?" he asked, knowing it was a stupid question but having to ask anyway.

"No," she said quietly. "That's all right. It's never easy for me." A tenderness in her tone, for, after all, he was her lover now and the badness of it was her own fault. She put her hands on his head, holding his face into the curve of her neck.

His cock limp and finished in her, he was ashamed of his inadequacy. All these years trapped in marriage, he had dreamed of great fucks with great women, how they would cherish his mighty cock—and he had ejaculated so prematurely she had had no chance at an orgasm.

Because he had fucked in anger, not in love.

Ignorant of his intention, she did not take alarm when he slid down the length of her body; not until she felt his hands parting her legs, his face pressing against her mount, did she cry out, struggling futilely to sit up, away from this strange assault.

It was too late. His mouth was on her, *his tongue was probing like a small, hot, irresistible bird, and no man had ever, had ever* . . . She could not allow it, she'd *never* be able to bear such a sweet probing of her tenderest flesh. But the resistance was only in her mind; her body opened and warmed to the irresistible flicker of his tongue as his head burrowed into her nest like a small, warm, greedy animal.

She gasped and locked her legs around his head. He had found the clitoris and was sucking it up, palpating it against the roof of his mouth. She groaned deeply, bucking up and down in an ecstasy of new sensation. The old bed shook with the violent movement. Her breath panted in small screams as she mounted instantaneously into a thrashing orgasm.

At first, in the gelid gash, he had tasted only his own come. Then, with a gush of liquid, he tasted *her*, a sweetly nutty flavor. He clung to her thrashing body, his teeth chittering insanely against the tiny nodule of clitoris; then he inhaled it in one great gulp. A salty taste now, that he drank greedily.

It was a pussy so much younger, sweeter, than Eleanor's; he hardly ever did Eleanor anymore, but this cunt he could eat forever. She was screaming somewhere far above him, but the world was her writhing pussy, fucking harder and harder against his face; she wanted him to eat it up, devour it forever. He tried valiantly to do as she wished.

An agony of orgasms, each ebbing only slightly before mounting higher into the next. So fiercely abandoned to her need, she was naked to him as she had never been naked to any man, not even Billy-Bob—for no man until now had done it to her like this.

His mouth left her; she moaned her loss as she grabbed frantically to keep his head where it belonged. But he was climbing up her, like climbing a ladder of flesh, and suddenly his great bird was where his tongue, so small and clever, had been. It was so enormous, in contrast, that her palpitating pussy expected to hurt, as it had hurt before; except this time it wasn't a hurting, only an utter ecstasy, for she was still coming, she would come forever until she died with the coming.

He rode her thrashing body as if he were riding a wild mare, fiercely exultant that he had set her reluctant flesh on fire. He could not fuck into such turbulence; he could only keep his cock plugged deep, the pulsating walls of her vagina stroking him willy-nilly into a second coming, milking him of everything he had left.

Slowly, with sensuous twitchings and murmurings, they subsided out of the giant stride of fucking until they lay still and exhausted. He tried to roll his weight off her, but her body crept after him. She shuddered as she pressed hard against his long body; she felt all pussy now, so sensitive and alive to his living, sensitive flesh. *And she had thought, "Pussy."*

They lay glued together, passion slowly ebbing to a tender residue of completion. After a time, she lifted her head to gaze into his face. Her eyes were seeing, her mouth tender.

"No man has ever done that to me," she said, finding it necessary to whisper the words because they were so fraught with great love. "No man. Not ever."

She placed a fingertip on his mouth, traced the softened line of his lip. She leaned to kiss him, her mouth softer than his. She could taste the smell of her pussy; it excited her, faintly but warmly, as it gave her the immediate sensory memory of what he had done to her with his mouth.

"I wouldn't have *let* you," she said, still whispering. "But I'm glad you did it. Do you understand that?"

"You were *something*," he said fondly. "Once you got

started." Then he had to ask, "Are you *really* glad we fucked?"

She laid her cheek on his chest, seeking the wiry brush of hairiness against her skin. She moved one hand to his crotch, to cradle warmly his cock, his balls. *For the first time, her mind had not flinched from those words, either*.

"I told you," she said, muffled against his chest. "Don't you believe me?"

"Yes," he said.

She pushed the words into speech, saying, "I love you. I love your . . . your cock, your balls, I love everything about you, your mouth, your cock, and all."

He laughed, because the words were tumbling over each other in her hurry to say them, and he put his hand on her mount to begin again the joyous fucking.

She sat up suddenly. "God, what time is it? I've got to get out of here."

He glanced at his watch. "You don't have to go yet."

"I don't dare be late . . ." She hovered over him, eyes watchful. "You didn't say it was . . . good for you. *Was* it good?"

He cupped his hand under the near breast. "God, yes!" he said. "It started out not so good, sure. But then . . ."

Simultaneously they laughed, and sighed with reminiscence. Her hand slipped from the ball sack to his cock, gripped it. "You have a beautiful cock. Beautiful. So *big!*"

Immediately, without pause for preparation or adjustment, they were fucking again. Fucking in rhythm this time, beginning slowly, pacing themselves, her body rocking gently under his steady thrust. Both were so absorbed, the squeal of the old bedsprings could not break their concentration.

She could *feel* him this time. She savored the length, the size, of his cock, how it crammed her full, the hot tip flicking and withdrawing against her cervix in the deepest fucking she had ever experienced. It hurt and felt good at once, a delicious half-hurt, half-ecstasy, she had never known with Hale.

"Beautiful cock," she murmured. "Beautiful cock, oh, a

74

beautiful cock . . ." and realized only belatedly that she was coming, sweet and long. Since he was not yet ejaculating, she could be luxurious in exploitation of the delicious sensation; until, realizing she was leaving him behind, in a panic at the thought of failing him, she began to fuck vigorously under him. Responding instantly to her urgency, his cock gushed a small, hard-drawn coming into her final orgasm.

"Now, *that's* fucking!" he said exultantly the moment they were finished. A lilt in the words, a self-congratulatory happiness that made her also happy. She was content, knowing that it was now indeed a true Adventure . . . an Adventure she would not have missed for anything in the world.

"Time to go," she whispered—*I always seem to be whispering,* she thought—and he replied, so satisfactorily, "Don't say it's time to go. It's never time to go even when it *is* time to go."

She could then say, "Next Thursday?" and he replied happily, "Same time, same place," as he hugged her with enthusiasm.

She had to make the first move to get out of bed, his hands lingering on her flesh in a final attempt to hold her back. She made herself get dressed though he remained where he was, unashamedly naked on top of the crumpled, come-dampened sheets.

She studied his body. Even now, limp and finished, his cock was long and weighty. If I had done what he wanted so badly, how would it have tasted in my mouth? she thought suddenly.

She was immediately seized by a revulsion at the weird idea. Hastily she said, "What are we going to do about these?" She fingered one corner of the top sheet.

"God, I hadn't thought about that," he said, sitting up abruptly. "We've always just taken them into town for laundering."

"I can wash them at home, bring 'em back next time," she suggested. "Come on, get up and help me fold them."

"Won't your husband . . . ?"

"Hale wouldn't know they weren't our sheets if I put them on his bed," she said confidently.

He consented to get dressed while she stripped the sheets. "Say," he said suddenly. "Can I call you?"

She paused to consider. "I suppose so," she said doubtfully. "I'm usually alone in the house during the daytime, now that the girls are off at camp." She regarded him silently. "Why would you need to call?"

"Probably wouldn't *need* to. I might just like to talk to you, that's all." He paused. "Of course, if something did come up, about Next Thursday, say . . ."

A wariness showed in her eyes. "Do you think something might come up?"

He faced her honestly. "No. I do not. If you think . . ."

"I'm sorry," she said quickly. "Just a woman's suspicious nature, I guess, that now that you've had what you wanted . . ."

He took her into his arms. "Listen. It's not like that," he said strongly. "You *know* that. Don't you?"

She nestled against his strong body. "Yes. I know it." Then, as though in despair: "I'll be thinking about you all week long."

"Yes," he said. "Me, too." Feeling her tremble in his arms, he knew he could take her again, this minute, on the now-bare mattress. No time for it, he knew in a reasonable corner of his mind. Still, the knowledge filled him with tenderness, so that he kissed her, one hand lingering against her breast. He could feel through the thin cloth that the nipple was taut under the stroke of his fingers.

"Don't get me started again," she warned laughingly, moving away. "We don't want to blow it the very first time, do we?"

He laughed with her, but took the opportunity to remark slyly, "Well, according to you, you don't *ever* want to blow it."

He had to explain it; she had never heard the term.

She was serious. "Do people . . . women . . . actually *do* that?"

"Sure," he said. "It's the first thing my wife ever did to me. *All* she would do until we were safely married."

Resisting the instinctive revulsion, she made herself try to visualize the act. She couldn't, not really, so then she had to say the next thing. "I suppose she still . . . blows you, then?"

"Sure," he said jauntily. "Eleanor *loves* it, she always has."

She suddenly did not want to think about taking his wife's place. Instead, an involuntary thought flashed through her mind; I could try it on Hale. Inside, where *he* could not hear, she laughed at the thought of how astonished Hale would be. After all these years, she'd never dare introduce such a radical new departure into their love-making. Hale would surely realize that she had learned it from another man.

She sighed. The double life. And suppose she made Hale put his mouth on her? She couldn't imagine him doing that, either.

They were happy together, even gay, on the way back to the rendezvous point. He unloaded his bicycle and stood, reluctant to depart, beside the station wagon. She looked into his face, so dear to her now.

"Until Next Thursday, then."

He put his hand on hers, where it rested on the car door, and repeated, "Until Next Thursday."

She did not start the engine, but sat watching him ride away. There was a proud lilt to the thought in her mind: *I fucked that man. I fucked him. And I am free at last to be all of me.*

The Man:

Eleanor, to his dismay, was home already, standing at the bar in the living room, fixing a scotch and soda.

"How'd it go today?" he asked, apprehensively ready for inquiry into his late arrival.

She did not turn to look at him. "We won, I got a new partner today. Want a drink?"

"Sure," he said, though, in the interest of weight control, he seldom took a drink during the week.

She gave him his glass, lifted hers in salute. He responded in kind, thinking: To Eleanor I am the same person who got out of bed with her this morning. The husband I've always been, devoted, faithful, reliable. Then, with unexpected sadness: We never know each other, do we?

He wondered, suddenly, what Eleanor thought of him. She had, after all, initiated the relationship, predicated on marriage to follow. They had been partners in parenthood, in the marriage, in his career.

As now, when Eleanor reminded him briskly, "Party tonight, remember. The Winslows."

Tab Winslow was the vice-president at the bank who would step into his heir-apparent shoes if ever he stumbled.

"Do we have to?" he asked, knowing the answer.

"Have we ever reneged?" Eleanor said, absently stating the obvious. "You don't want them speculating about why we're not present and accounted for, do you?"

"I suppose not. Though what in the world they could find to speculate on, about *us*, I don't know."

Her voice was forceful. "Don't forget for one minute that Tab Winslow is after your job. He'd do anything to be standing in line ahead of you when the time comes. You know it. So don't give him an opening by ducking their invitations."

"Yeah, the Old Man's used Tab for years to keep me toeing the mark," he said wryly.

"Don't think Daddy wouldn't pass you over, either, if he believed it was in the best interests of the bank." It was a serious warning. "He was remarking at lunch, last Tuesday, that you had arrived at the dangerous age for a man. A lot of good men, he said, go off in weird ways at about forty-five or fifty. Said he's seen it happen too many times."

Every Tuesday without fail, she had lunch downtown with her father.

"I'm not forty-five yet," he said reasonably, even as the panicked awareness of this afternoon's fucking fluttered in his stomach. He gulped at the drink, moved to fix another.

"Don't rush it. It'll be a long evening," she said. "You know you'll wind up playing poker, the men always do at Tab's house."

"I've been taking Tab's money for years," he grunted. "Well, I suppose I'd better get my shower."

He had lived so long under Eleanor's tutelage that he didn't even resent it anymore, he realized. But then, he thought as he stripped off the shorts and T-shirt, she was the one person he could always count on his side. She concealed nothing from him, not even the luncheon intelligence from her father . . . information he had turned to profitable use more than once.

His thoughts shifted as he studied his lean, fit body in Eleanor's full-length mirror. *By God, I fucked her up the wall*, he congratulated himself. So cold to start with, letting me in about two inches. But then . . . she just went wild, that's all. I've sure as hell ruined her for her husband, or anybody else, he thought complacently. The husband couldn't be much, anyway, or she wouldn't have been looking.

His masculine mind, he realized, was treating her sordidly again. It's not fair, he told himself sternly, just because she wanted to fuck me.

Men seem to think that way about women, he reflected, remembering too many locker-room conversations. He, at least, had never bragged about *his* women. Yet, in his bachelor days, he had never considered marrying any one of the various girls who had taken off their clothes in his apartment. As though, somehow, their generous gesture had barred any serious involvement.

Only Eleanor, who wouldn't let him touch her until the wedding night.

To rescue his thoughts from self-criticism, he made himself remember the tenderness—the love—that had been between them this afternoon after lust had been satisfied. He was risking a lot for her—everything, in fact—so she *does* count, he told himself. She counts more than she knows.

Under the shower, a new thought: What if, by chance, she happened to be at the party tonight? No reason why she should, she never had been, he could undoubtedly list the guests off the top of his head. But *what if* . . . ?

They would look secretly at each other across the room, the so-recent love-making warm in their loins; and her mere presence would instill a special quality into the party ambience. She might even find a moment to touch him . . .

Under the warm flow of water, he was beginning to get a new erection. It would not do to come into the bedroom with a hard-on; Eleanor might be there.

Why had they never chanced to meet, growing up in this small city? She had said in passing that her husband was an attorney; they undoubtedly belonged to the small elite of the city, as he and Eleanor belonged. He had never, to his knowledge, had any dealings with the man.

With the wandering of his mind, the hard-on had subsided by the time he emerged from the bathroom. No danger, anyway—Eleanor remained elsewhere in the house. He glanced at the phone, yearning to hear *her* voice.

He recoiled. What if her husband answered? God, maybe the Old Man was right, saying he had arrived at a weird time of life. Possessed by the random desires of a new lover, he seemed unable to take his mind away from *her*. Wonderful to feel so, after so many years. *Dangerous* to feel so, if he allowed it to take the name of action.

He was grateful when Eleanor entered the bedroom and began preparing to take her usual tub bath.

He had long been aware that Judy, Tab Winslow's wife, had a thing for him. It was, he knew, compounded of sexual attraction, envy of his position ahead of her husband's at the bank, and jealousy of Eleanor for being born the star-crowned daughter of the bank president.

The trouble was, Judy was one hell of a good-looking woman. Small, with delicate features, she was wearing a knee-length white dress with a cleavage terribly indiscreet for their staid circle. She was nearly always daring in her dress, but got away with it because she was Judy.

At the door, he made the obligatory move to kiss her cheek, but, as usual, Judy gave him her mouth instead, pouting slightly that he had not assumed it as a right.

Her lips were soft, warming; she gave him a startled glance as she withdrew from the discreet embrace. He wondered if he had revealed to her something he had not shown before.

"Well, well, well, so here we are," Tab said heartily, advancing with outstretched hand as though they did not spend every working day together. "I hope you brought the large money tonight. I intend to get better than even for the last time."

Tab was a bluff and hearty man, his shrewdness showing only in his small eyes. He had always thought, disapprovingly, that Tab looked more like a used-car salesman than a banker. But his whiskey-drinking, poker-playing image, betrayed in the faint pattern of broken veins over his cheekbones, had not prevented a steady accumulation of power and responsibility.

He shook Tab's hand, thinking with secret glee: And what did *you* do with your afternoon off, Tab, old boy? Fuck a good woman, like I did?

As he moved on to the bar to mix his third drink of the evening, he found himself trying to visualize Tab and Judy in the sack. Small as she was, the bulk of her husband would absolutely smother her. Tab, so heavy in the hips, would be ponderous in his clumsy drive into her flesh.

He looked across the room at Judy, to find her eyes brightly on his. Once or twice in their long acquaintance, she had given him covert signals . . . signals he had ignored. Now he prudently shifted his gaze and moved to merge with the group of guests chatting amiably beside the French windows. He was aware, however, when Judy, ostensibly pursuing her duties as hostess, joined the group to stand at his side.

Women, when their blood is hot, can sense when a man has been with a woman, he thought profoundly. It makes the male somehow more attractive to them.

He noticed, next, that Eleanor had approached, to stand protectively at his other elbow as he talked with one of his regular bank customers. Turning away, he winked to let Eleanor know that he was aware, also . . . aware and amused.

Eleanor and I, he thought smugly, we're used to women putting the moves on me. It's because I've kept myself in so much better shape than most men my age. He was comfortably aware of his lean body under the loose-fitting drape of the sports coat, the elegant slacks. A body so recently well-fucked, by a marvelous woman. *She* has seen me only in bicycling shorts, he remembered abruptly, wishing that she could see him now.

Quite the predictable party for their set: eight couples, making two bridge tables for the ladies while the men retired to Tab's aggressively masculine den for cutthroat poker.

Eleanor hated playing bridge with "amateurs," as she scornfully termed them. But of course, with her impeccable social sense, she always played with a careful deprecation of her normal skills at the game that was the passion of her life. Eleanor was advancing steadily toward becoming a life master. She would have made it already if she hadn't been always reluctant to be away from home longer than overnight, which confined her to the smaller, regional tournaments.

Once, conscientiously, he had taken up the game under her tutelage, with the idea of playing as partners. It had not worked; with Eleanor so impatient in teaching, he sensed that she would prefer selecting her own partners, instead of being tied down to her husband. For her sake, he had abandoned the attempt.

He was, he realized, more acutely aware than usual tonight of the people around him. Especially the women, mentally comparing them to the woman of this afternoon. Even Judy, he decided, didn't measure up, though there would certainly be rewards in her; he could imagine how enthusiastic she must be in fucking. Nor was he at all surprised to find himself at her right hand for dinner, with Eleanor far down the table. He was, after all, the presumed next president of the bank where her husband worked.

Deliberately, as a secret amusement, he punished Judy by devoting most of his attention to the plump, comfortable woman at his right, who raised poodles and talked only about raising poodles. Immediately following dinner, he was safely ensconced with the other men at the poker table in the den, the women beyond the closed door. He bought a hundred dollars' worth of chips and settled down to take Tab Winslow's money.

Which, he reminded himself, was always easy to do, given decent cards. Tab was as open as a book; you only had to read him backward. He wondered, suddenly, if such a transparent man could ever be successful as the president of a large bank. Then and there, he made the decision that, when he himself became president, Tab Winslow would have gone as far as he'd go in the organization.

He was pleased with himself. It was how the Old Man would operate, making relevant decisions far in advance of events.

He won over two hundred dollars, and during the final get-together with the ladies for a nightcap, while Tab Winslow was being jovially loud about his losses, Judy

Winslow said conspiratorially at his elbow, "You won, didn't you?"

He turned to her. "Yeah, won a little," he admitted.

Her eyes were direct, but her mouth belied her daring by the bite of small, white teeth on her lower lip. "You're always better than Tab, aren't you?" Then she added, "At poker."

"Nearly always," he said with a casual shrug. "At poker."

He sensed that in her next words she meant to risk a dangerous step further. But Eleanor was beside him now, saying warmly, "I'd certainly have lost tonight if Judy hadn't been my partner. Judy, you play so *well.*"

He left the party knowing that one woman had sensed in him a difference—a vulnerability. And, he added warningly, I mustn't discount Eleanor, either. She was right there when she needed to be there.

"That Judy, she is one good-looking woman, isn't she?" he remarked casually as he sat on the side of the bed taking off his loafers. "Great hostess, too."

Deliberately, in order to defuse any possible jealousy, he had given Eleanor an opening.

She took it. "Judy seems to have decided all over again to have the hots for you," she said from her side of the bed. "I thought I had discouraged that sort of thing quite effectively, a long time ago."

"You really think so?" he asked in a tone of mild interest. "Judy doesn't bother me."

Eleanor gave him a level look. "I *know* so. And, as you well know, I'm never wrong when I say a woman is dangerously attracted to you."

"Oh, Eleanor! You're just being jealous again. Judy did look beautiful tonight, you'll have to admit."

Eleanor said thoughtfully, "She seemed to be under some sort of strain. I wonder if Tab is running around on her again."

"Again?" he said in surprise. "You mean, he's jumped the reservation before?"

"Don't you remember, five years ago, when Daddy had to have a little talk with Tab about his private life?"

"No," he said slowly. "I don't think you ever told me that. I'd have remembered, for sure."

She nodded. "He had a girl on the side, and it began to look as though he might actually divorce Judy and marry her, young as she was. Until Daddy read him the riot act."

He was alarmed. "You mean to tell me, after a thing like that, Tab is still a candidate?"

"Well, Daddy felt that Tab was probably over the hump —and he'd never *dare* risk it again."

Disturbed, he stood up and began taking off his shirt. "The Old Man would never give *me* a second chance," he said bitterly. "You can bet on that."

She regarded him blandly. "*Tab* isn't his son-in-law," she pointed out. "He's not *family*."

When he got into bed, Eleanor moved to him. From long familiarity, he knew that she wished nothing more than the reassurance of slipping into sleep with her mouth on him. So Eleanor had indeed been aware of . . . *something*. He was grateful to Judy Winslow for the diversion she had provided.

So disturbed, he could only gradually relax as he yielded his body to his wife's need for the reassurance of the oldest habit of their life together. But then, with the first gentle response to the sensation of her sucking, he found in his mind the new woman of his heart, the great woman he had fucked so greatly only this afternoon.

Turning from reminiscence of today, he began dreaming in anticipation of next week. He would *make* her taste him with her mouth. He would not touch her where it counted until she had consented to do what Eleanor was doing at this moment.

Once conquered by his demand, she would *love* it. She'd go wild, the way she had gone wild today with his mouth eating her pussy; and, again, he would be the first man to whom she had ever done that thing. As he was the first man, this afternoon, to do it to her.

He settled himself into the fantasy of Next Thursday as Eleanor's warm mouth sucked him gently, gently, into a half-sleeping repose that was yet deeply erotic. When he

85

came, at long last but without effort, slow and sweet and forever, he did not know whether the real mouth, or the dream mouth, had brought such sweet consummation to his flesh.

The Woman:

Her party was on Friday night, a neighborhood cookout, the men gathered around the outdoor barbecue, the women clustered in the kitchen to do the salad and make the French fries, gossiping among themselves as the men were laughing and gossiping outside.

Only when the two groups merged was she aware, with frightening abruptness, that she had been catapulted into a new world.

The event that cued her attention was the sight of her best friend, Rosemary Dobbs, standing with Julian Peabody. The two had paused quite casually for a moment's chat in the shadow of the big oak beside the back door. Rosemary was coming from the house, hands filled with salt and pepper shakers, while Julian, ostentatiously rattling the ice in his glass, had ambled toward the kitchen seeking a fresh drink.

They spoke only briefly, standing quite apart, Rosemary listening with a smile to whatever Julian was telling her. But then Rosemary, lifting her eyes, swept the crowd to seek her husband and found him standing with back turned, laughing at a joke. *In that moment,* she saw in utter shock, *Rosemary touched Julian's bare arm.* Her fingertips brushed only lightly, quickly, then she left immediately, Julian looking hungrily after her.

Unmistakable. She knew, as well as if her friend had confided in her, that Rosemary and Julian were lovers. In that outwardly casual chat, their next meeting had been arranged.

With newly opened eyes she turned to survey the crowd. Harry Barger stood with his arm around Betty Black as he talked jovially with Betty's husband. Well, it *was* an affectionate group. However, the manner in which Betty leaned against Harry's arm made their contact too intimate, too revealing. *They, too, had fucked.* And, watching Bill Black's face, she knew that he was aware of it.

Innocent, she told herself fiercely. I've been as innocent as a babe in arms. I *know* these people—at least, I thought I did—known them for two or three or ten years. I just never *saw.*

What if *he* were here? Would we act like Rosemary and Julian, chatting casually yet secretly, betrayed to a watching eye only by the temptation of a lingering touch? If *I* can see it, others must also; they simply ignore it, live with it, accept it as the way people are.

We're not like that, she told herself fiercely. We're different, we have created a separate world for *our* love. We have no wish to flaunt it, as Rosemary flaunted her signal that she knows the size, the feel, of Julian's bird. She will have that bird in her nest again before the week is out.

She was trembling inside with the realization that, all her married life, she had been blind to so much going on about her in this society of unrecognized—until now—secret sexual signals and hidden ploys.

In her need to deny the revelation, she told herself: We'll keep *our* love where it belongs. We won't allow it to become part of our everyday life, as these brazen people do. I don't ever want to be at a party with *him,* see *him* shaking hands with my husband, telling mutual male jokes, knowing all the while he has fucked Hale's wife.

With her warm memories of this afternoon, her chilled awareness of the sexual undercurrents about her, she felt entirely separate and alone. I've got to make myself join the party, she warned herself, or else someone will see *me.*

Forcing a facade of participation, she merged with the nearest group, accepting a fresh glass, talking with feverish intensity. The masquerade was promptly jeopardized when suddenly she felt a male hand clasp her forearm.

She turned sharply to see that it was Paul, a short, rather fat man who was always touching her. Always with sexual intent, she realized with a fresh sense of horror at her previous innocence. *He wants everybody to believe he's had me*, she thought clearly. No way he *could* have me, he knows that, so he's content if only people will believe . . .

The perception blazing through her mind was as real as if he had told her the blunt truth. Sharply she said, "Don't touch me, Paul. I *hate* being touched like that."

Nearby heads turned inquisitively. She couldn't help that; she had to free herself from the trap.

Paul said in an aggrieved voice, as though somehow deprived of a right; "Well, I'm *sorry*," and walked away.

She felt desolate, exposed. I'm a stranger to these old neighbors, she thought miserably. I have never shared their games. She realized, then, that serious passes had not been made at her because the men's instincts had sensed her unavailability. She not only didn't know the rules; she hadn't even known a game was being played.

And Hale? she thought, her mind turning apprehensively to her husband. She scanned the crowd, to find him, glass in hand, telling a joke to a circle of men. A dirty story, she could read from the grinning anticipation of his audience.

There was, she saw, one woman among them—Petey Armbruster—and she recognized quite clearly that Petey, who had carried that silly nickname all the way out of grammar school because she had been such a tomboy, was yearning for Hale. She laughed more heartily than anyone when the punch line came, thumping a fist against Hale's shoulder in ostensible delight.

Hale, she was happy to see, remained oblivious, chuckling quietly at his story-telling success; then, rattling his glass, he moved to replenish his drink. He did not notice that Petey followed . . . though, politely, he fixed Petey a drink also.

Strange to suspect her husband of participating in the social sex game. But they're *all* playing, always *have* been, she told herself, observing the glint of teeth in seductive smiles, the sparkle of eyes, the casual, drifting movements toward and away from each other which were not at all casual, but seeking, always seeking. So why should she hold Hale immune, as she had been immune?

Maybe everybody here has fucked everybody else at one time or another, she reflected. They all know it, but never, never, will anyone admit it, to themselves or to each other. While, all the time, I've stood apart, and no man has dared to seek in my stupid innocence a partner for illicit sex.

One man did, though, she told herself in a rush of warmth. Only this afternoon, we were together. But we're different, we are ourselves, our love is truly secret because it is isolated from husbands and wives and friends and children.

Warm now, fulfilled; and suddenly, glowing in her mind, she knew that Next Thursday she would taste his bird with her mouth. His *cock*, she corrected herself fiercely. Never again use that silly euphemism.

She gazed away into the farther darkness, dreaming of it. She'd have to force herself, she knew even in this moment of reckless euphoria. But he lusted for her mouth, and she would do it for *him*, her lover; she would do it for love even if she hated doing it. Her tenderest flesh pulsed suddenly, as though his cock waited poised at the entrance to her nest. She hoped the tiny shiver of orgasm was as deeply hidden as the feeling itself.

He can do that to me, too, she thought happily. She had always been slow with Hale, often unable to get to orgasm because Hale, thinking only of his steady pumping, never paused to feel and respond to her needs.

As if, to my husband, I'm nothing more than a warm hole, she thought, when I'm his wife, he *loves* me, as far as he knows he's the only man—with the exception of Billy-Bob—who has had me.

She gazed across the party at Hale, wondering, for the first time in their twenty years together, if the memory of Billy-Bob preceding him in her flesh had affected his love-making all these years.

"Well! *You* look a million miles away. Dare tell me what you're thinking?"

Julian. She gazed at him from the distance of her new perspective, thinking, He's a terribly attractive man. I'll bet he's fucked nearly every woman here. Except me.

"It might be *too* much of a surprise," she said lightly. "You'd be utterly scandalized, Julian." She was gratified by the flare of interest in his eyes. She had meant it as a come-on, perversely seeking to strike the same sexual spark that Rosemary had so obviously lighted in this man.

Satisfied, she walked away before Julian had mustered a riposte. Moved by the affection, if not lust, she had discovered in her soul for her husband, she paused at Hale's side and touched his arm, saying softly, "Hello, Husband." She was warmed by the quickness with which he turned, his welcoming smile.

"Having a good time?" he asked solicitously.

"Of course," she said. "This is quite a bunch we've gathered around us, isn't it?"

He said comfortably, "Good people. I enjoy it every time we get together."

Protected by her husband as she watched the circulation of the crowd, she felt forgiving of her previous censures. They are, each one, two or three different people inside themselves, she thought, just as I am. I stand beside my husband, touching him, feeling warm and *together;* yet only a few hours ago, when I held another man in my arms, Hale was a million miles away and a million years absent.

They seek love, also, she thought profoundly. These women lust, as I have lusted, for a cock that is a stranger to their flesh. And the men . . . The men prowl after strange women, yet they want to come home to their cave, where the woman they can always count on is waiting.

Or, perhaps, just returned from her own female prowling.

Soon now, within a couple of hours, in her bed she could give her thoughts to *him,* shaping in her mind a beautiful Next Thursday in which she would "do" him, as he so oddly termed it. And even if Hale, stirred into desire by tonight's display of affection, came into her, his cock would not disturb the fantasy.

The Two:

Thursday morning it was raining.

It made her fretful. She was reluctant, anyway, to go to her lover today; last night Hale had desired sex, and it did not seem right to be with two men within such a short span of time. She had accepted that sooner or later it would have to happen . . . but not so soon.

It had not bothered her nearly so much to go from lover to husband, as from husband to lover, and that didn't make sense, either.

With tomorrow in her mind, she had endured Hale —yet, in fear of overreacting, she had held tomorrow at bay. So, this morning, she experienced a strong sense of relief as she waited for *his* telephone call canceling their assignation.

An unsatisfactory sort of rain, as doubtful and unstable as her mind. At nine o'clock the skies were overcast, the rain coming down with an all-day steadiness; by ten, only showers, far more typical of spring weather, with patches of blue sky showing. Still the telephone did not ring, and by eleven another freshet had settled in.

She wandered about the house, unable to settle down to wifely tasks. I'm not cut out for this sort of intrigue, she thought, rueful of the comfortable life she had known for so many easy years.

To cap the irritation of her restlessness, Rosemary arrived for coffee, saying cheerfully that she couldn't stand the kids for another minute without some adult conversation, not on a rainy day like this, and there might be a phone call for her while she was here, she hoped she wouldn't mind.

The sight of her best friend reminded her forcibly of the revelation of last week's cookout. She felt an impulse to confide in Rosemary about *her* Adventure, simply to see if Rosemary would reciprocate. Firmly she suppressed the dangerous idea and went into the kitchen to make coffee. Rosemary remained comfortably seated on the sofa, lifting her voice to carry on the chatter that she called conversation.

"I wish I'd enrolled the kids in summer camp, like you did. But we decided to save the money for a Caribbean cruise, instead of our usual mountain vacation. *They are driving me crazy. He* doesn't have to put up with them the livelong day like I do."

The phone rang. Before she could react, Rosemary had snatched up the living-room extension. She stood frozen in the kitchen doorway, positive it was *him* calling. How in the world could she explain a phone call from a strange man?

"Oh, hi!" Rosemary said blithely, then, unnecessarily, to her, "It's for me." She listened for a long minute, nodding in unconscious agreement. "Why, yes, I think I could manage that," she said enthusiastically. "I'd be *delighted*, as a matter of fact." Rosemary was still watching her in the doorway as she added in a sharper tone, "Well, OK, *count* on it, then," and hung up.

She brought the coffee. As Rosemary added Sweet'n'Low, she said casually, "Old Miss Murphy has been after me for *weeks* to tend a booth at the charity dog show. I had to agree just to get her off my back."

She was astounded by the facile lie; even more astounded when Rosemary drank her coffee without ceremony and stood up, saying, "I'd better get back before they *completely* wreck the house. Thanks for the coffee and the time out from the domestic wars."

At the door, putting on her raincoat, she remarked, gazing out at the weather, "You're lucky, to stay home on a day like this. *I've* got to go out in this mess and meet with the dog show committee."

Alone again, she felt an unreasonable resentment. She knew, as well as if she had been listening on an extension, that Rosemary, relying on her innocence, had come over to use her telephone in making another assignation with

Julian. She was quite sure she'd never feel quite the same way toward her best friend.

Her mind made a wry shift. Had she not stood frozen with fear that Rosemary would hear *his* voice when she snatched up the telephone? Feeling even more strongly that she could not possibly see him today, she considered calling the bank where he worked. He must surely get many phone calls in the way of business, women customers as well as men. But, quite sure her voice would betray their secret to his secretary, she did not dare.

She waited in vain until it was too late to do her grocery shopping beforehand. Which meant, she thought wistfully, we'll have that much less time together. He probably wouldn't come, anyway, in this rain; he probably had not called because of an assumption that she would understand. She knew, as she knew she must make the effort to meet him, that she would wait too long, miserable but stubborn, on the side of the road before deciding he didn't mean to come.

It was raining hard again, blurring the windshield as she drove with care directly to the rendezvous point. Her heart lifted when it slowed to a drizzle, but by the time she had arrived it was coming down heavily again.

Sure enough, he wasn't there. Chilled, she sat huddled into herself, knowing how stupid she was to be waiting on the side of a country road for a man with too much common sense to come out in the rain. There was in her not the slightest trace of lust.

She couldn't believe her eyes when she saw him, head down against the rain, coming on the bicycle. She had assumed, if he arrived at all, it would be in a car. He stopped beside her window, water streaming down his face.

"For God's sake, put the bicycle in the back and get in," she said, laughing with a suddenly light heart as she gave him the cluster of keys.

He hurried to do her bidding, then slid drenched into the seat beside her. "That's a damn cold rain for this time of year," he said in greeting.

"Why didn't you call?" she said, gazing at him tenderly. "All morning I expected you to call and say it would be best to put it off."

He grinned, wiping his wet face with a wet hand. "Did you think I'd do that, when it will be another whole week before I could see you again?"

"I expected you, at least, to use your car."

He shook his head. "I never go anywhere in the car on Thursday. It's my day for a long bicycle ride, remember?"

It was all suddenly very funny; laughter bubbled in her. "How in the world are you going to explain coming home drenched to the bone?"

"Oh, I've been caught out in the rain before," he said gaily. "You don't happen to have a towel back there, do you?"

"Only the sheets I was bringing back to the cabin."

He pulled the clinging T-shirt over his head, futilely wiped his chest with it. "Better than nothing. Reach back and get me one."

While she got the sheet, he wriggled out of the shorts. Chuckling, he said, "In case you haven't noticed, lady, there's a naked man in your station wagon."

She leaned to touch him familiarly. "I noticed." She began rubbing his chest with the dry cloth. "God, you'll catch your death of a summer cold."

She began drying his upper body tenderly, rubbing his chest and back and belly, then down his legs and into the crotch, with him half-rising so she could get the sheet under him.

"Come on, let's get going," he said impatiently. "We're running late as it is."

She stopped the movement of her hands. Soberly she said, "Suppose this heavy station wagon gets stuck up there? It's been raining all morning, and the road to the cabin will be terribly slick."

"It's fairly rocky," he protested. "Listen, I didn't come out in this miserable weather to sit in a car and smooch."

"Even if we don't get stuck, the car will have mud all

over it," she added, just realizing it herself. "How would I ever explain a muddy station wagon?"

"Take it to a car wash before you go home."

"In a pouring rain? What would they think, a woman getting her car washed in a pouring rain?"

"What do you *care* what they think?" he said irritably. "Why do you drive such a gas guzzler, anyway? *Nobody* owns a big car anymore."

"Hale figured it out," she said seriously. "With the discount you get with a big car, I can drive nearly ten years before the gas saved by a small car would make up the difference."

"Good for old Hale," he grunted. "That doesn't help us out *now*." He stared at her challengingly. "So what do we do? Sit here on the side of the road and *look* at each other?" He felt aggrieved enough to bring up something that had been on his mind all week. "You won't even go down on a fellow, for God's sake."

Repelled by the bald words, she felt her voice tremble. "We can't stay here, either. We ought to drive on, at least . . ." She started the engine, and drove slowly through dwindling rain. It wasn't going at all as she had fantasied.

They would be in the cabin, of course; him stretched naked on the bed with her kneeling over him, stroking his cock with both hands, admiring it, loving it—then she would bend down her head and . . . She had not been able to visualize the act itself, the actual sensation, but she would do it, surely she would do it . . .

She shivered. He said solicitously, "Are you cold? It's a miserable day to be out in, I should have called . . ."

She gave him a wan smile. "I really *wanted* to be here. I wanted to . . ." She couldn't say it. She felt a reckless impulse to take this damn station wagon up the twisting dirt road, no matter if they did get stuck and had to call a wrecker, no matter if she did bring the car home spattered with mud.

In the fork of the byroad they took into the hills was a cluster of trees. She turned off, intending to go on to the cabin. But, courage failing her, she took the beaten path into the picnic area inside the oak grove. Here, at least, the car was hidden from prying eyes. With it raining harder again, surely no one would come along to use the picnic tables.

She turned off the engine, looked at her lover wrapped naked in the white sheet. Deliberately she tilted the steering wheel up out of the way, slid the seat back. She took off her blouse, exposing her breasts to his gaze. Today, she had not worn a bra.

He felt his breath catch at sight of her inviting nakedness. He leaned his face into her breasts, catching a nipple under his tongue as her arms cradled his head.

She began to talk in a voice throaty with passion. "I want to do *that*, my love, I want to do everything you want me to do. It's just that . . . I've never *thought* of doing it, it seems *nasty* to me . . ." She was shaking with the intensity of feeling.

In surprise, he raised his mouth from her breast. "*Nothing* is dirty when it's between two people who love each other. I did *you*, remember? I *loved* doing you."

Her arms tightened. "*Do* you love me?"

He felt the hesitation in his mind, hoped it did not show in his voice. "Yes. Of course." He laughed softly. "It wasn't *love* that was in my mind, first time I saw you. But . . . I do love you."

With both hands, she lifted his face away from her naked breasts to gaze deeply into his eyes.

He had to make her do it now, he realized. If he failed to push her over the edge of reluctance, something irrevocable would become lost; they would never reach the farther edge of their lust, their love.

Softly he said, "Remember how it felt with my mouth on you? It feels that good for me, too." He hesitated. Then he said, "I want you to do to me what you've never done to any man, not even your husband. That way, you'll *prove* how much you love me."

Her mouth trembled. "But what if . . ."

"I promise. I won't come in your mouth," he said

quickly, thinking wryly of that silly joke about the world's three most-broken promises.

She teetered on the brink of action. He held his breath, waiting. His cock was jerking between his legs, demanding greedily the warmth of her mouth. Slowly, but with a firm pressure, she pushed him back, half leaning, against the door.

They were in a secret room of the rain, as private and hidden as in the cabin. He felt it so, she felt it so, as her hands removed the sheet from over his loins, bringing the rampant cock of his being into the sight of her eyes.

As she had fantasied, she took both hands to encircle it, holding it jerking in her warm palms while she crooned, "He's so beautiful, he's the most beautiful cock in the world, so *big*, so *long*, so *beautiful*."

It was, she saw in this heightened state of sensuousness, indeed a beautiful thing. The bulging head glowed a lovely rose-pink, a drop of moisture stood in the eye. Even with his hairiness, a delicate flush dwelled in the thin skin sheathing the shaft. It was as sensitive and responsive as the cock of a boy.

As she crooned over it, feeling it warm and strong in her hands, she told herself: I will lap up that bead of moisture with my tongue. Tasting it, I will know the taste of *him*. Still, something in her held back. Terrible if her stomach should roil, unforgivable.

The weight of his hand pressed at the back of her neck. "No," she said. "Don't force me."

He took away his hand, though he wished fiercely to crush her mouth into his loins, plunging his cock deeply into her throat. *Come*, by God, *come*.

He lifted his hand, freeing her from the pressure. So now she had to do as she had promised. Her jaws tightening, with the tip of her tongue, she lapped as tentatively as a cat tasting a suspicious substance. A strange taste, *strange* . . . she lapped again, curling her tongue slowly around the head. She felt him tremble in response, his tilting hips thrusting his cock forward, pleading for her mouth, and so she closed her lips firmly about the bulbous, rose-pink head.

Startled by the strangely rubbery texture, she withdrew as quickly. He surged, both hands grabbing at her head, holding it firmly as he rammed his cock deeply into her throat. Struggling frantically, she began to choke. His hands soothed her, his voice saying falsely, "I'm sorry, I couldn't help it, I . . ."

It was her dream, wasn't it? It was *happening;* and so, of her own will, she accepted his cock, too deep but refusing, this time, to back off. Her throat began a compulsive swallowing as she sucked desperately at the throbbing shaft.

He sighed, and she knew that she was pleasing him. Even as she concentrated on satisfying his male desires, she began to experiment with her own sensations, moving up to pulsate her lips against the head, biting tenderly with the edges of her teeth, then sliding slowly again down the shaft. She wasn't sure whether she liked the taste of it, the shape; but her hips were writhing in an unconscious gathering toward orgasm.

She was on her knees, crouched over him, wholly absorbed in the task of giving him pleasure. She did not know it, but her mouth was warmer now, softer; she was sucking hard, moving up and down rapidly, because she *wanted* him to come. If she felt him coming, she would surely come also.

She felt his hand in her crotch under the skirt, rubbing at her furry nest with tender persistence. She was fucking against his probing finger, she had gone too far now, he was over the edge and she was over the edge, and *he had lied, he was coming in her mouth, nasty, dirty come* . . .

Fucking her mouth, his cock was mindless, animal, uncaring of her sudden gagging. She felt the rising pulse of his ejaculation, she tried to scream but her mouth was too full, when she tried to get away, even in the midst of her own orgasm, he would not let her escape. But, in her panicked reaction, he could not hold her to it. Only inches away, panting in hyperventilation, with horrified eyes, she watched the lumpy white stuff pumping out, to ooze down the thick sides in a lava flow of semen.

Something reckless in her whispered bravely, Have it all now. *All*. With a groan, she yawned wide her jaws and plunged upon him again. He was still coming. It flooded her taste buds with the taste of oysters, a deep sea smell. So utterly satisfying, she clung to his cock like a limpet until it began to droop in completion.

She rose up to gaze into his face. The question that needed such a full answer trembled on her lips. "Did I . . . did I do you good?"

Feeling a great tenderness, he pulled her up so he could put his mouth on her bruised, softened mouth, wanting, in a strange self-gratification, to taste his cock on her lips. She has sucked no other man's cock, he told himself in great clarity and satisfaction.

"Yes," he said.

A simple, one-word answer, but it satisfied her. Lovingly, he said, "Did *you* like it?"

She sat up to think about it. "I don't know," she confessed. "It was strange, exciting . . ."

He chuckled. "If it excited you, you liked it." He held her cheek in one palm. "Next time, at the cabin, we'll do sixty-nine. That's a whole different sensation."

She had heard about sixty-nine, had only half understood because she had not wanted to think about it. *Innocent* . . . so damn innocent, and liking too much being that way.

"Do a lot of people do that . . . go down on each other?" she asked, and honestly resented his laughter.

"I don't know about other people. I just don't believe that you and I are going to invent something new at this late date in the history of the human race."

"You know, I've been blind to people all my life," she said suddenly. "I was at a cookout Friday night, and it was like being in a whole different world. People think about sex all the time, don't they, somewhere in the back of their minds? Why, my best friend made a date with another woman's husband right in front of God and everybody."

100

He laughed at her. "I don't know about your crowd, but my crowd goes on like that all the time. Nobody thinks anything about it . . . as long as it's kept undercover."

She was serious. "But why haven't I *seen* it before? It makes me feel silly to know that all these years . . ."

He was touched by her confidence. "Are you glad I gave you a new pair of eyes?"

She grasped at his hand, kissed the palm. "You've given me so much more."

He grinned. "A whole new world. We'll explore it together."

She nestled against him, content inside the car, made secret by the isolating rain. The windshield, the side windows, had become fogged with the heat of their breaths, so that she could not actually see the rain anymore, only feel it.

"Yes," she whispered. "You will be all the men I've ever dreamed about; for you, I will be all the women."

They kissed again, their hands moving, exploring. They were silent, intent upon sensation as their passion began to rise anew.

He turned half around to look into the back of the station wagon. "I need to fuck you now. Let's get back there, where we can stretch out . . ."

"There isn't room, with the bicycle," she said practically.

"Hell, I'll take the bicycle *out*." Recklessly he flung open the door, piled out naked into the rain. She laughed, watching him run around to let down the door.

With a wild impulse of her own, she took off her skirt and went out into the rain also, laughing as she ran to him. His hands grabbed at her. She fled away, teasing, running into the woods. He pounded after her, yelling with glee. She slipped and almost fell, but his hands saved her from the mud. They stood, embracing, their rain-slick bodies merging feverishly. He was saying, "I'll fuck you right here, right now," as he bent her down fiercely to fuck her on the wet ground, and she was frightened that he would, and afraid that he wouldn't.

In a last-minute refuge of caution, he picked her up in

his arms, saying, "Come on, silly woman, where you can get fucked *right*."

The bicycle out of the way, they climbed into the back of the station wagon, shivering, now that passion and glee had ebbed, from the chill wetness.

He recovered the damp sheet from the front seat and dried her with half of it, while she dried him with the other half. Between them they spread the other sheet over the foam-rubber padding installed so the children could ride comfortably in the back without being confined to seats. They curled into each other and she began to kiss him, slowly, lingeringly, saying between kisses, "What do you want me to be now? *Who* do you want me to be? Anybody you've ever dreamed about, Cleopatra or Lauren Bacall, that *Ten* girl, any woman in the world."

"Be *you*," he said in contentment. "That's all I need. *You.*"

He was ready to come on top. Dissatisfied with his answer, she forestalled him, whispering, "Then let me. *You* do what *I* want."

"If that's how you like it," he said dreamily, feeling no great lust at the moment.

She sat up, gazing down on him. "Look at that lazy thing," she said chidingly, fondling his cock. "He thinks he's had it, doesn't he?"

She was exploring now, inside herself as well as with his flesh, feeling the exhilaration, and yet the fear, of being free to do exactly as she pleased. I've always just laid down for Hale, she thought. Because that's all he ever wanted. But this man, this lover . . .

With a stroke of triumph in her soul, she found herself wishing Rosemary could see her now; Rosemary, who thought her so naive that she could take illicit phone calls before her very eyes.

"Little does he know," she crooned, stroking him with her hand. Bringing her head down, she put her mouth on him.

Different this time, more purposeful, because she was focused on arousing him to full erection. She felt herself as the all-powerful maker of sex, no longer merely the acquiescent female. As though she had done it a thousand times, she manipulated his cock with tongue and clever fingers, advancing and retreating, teasing when teasing was the right thing, making it stiffen until, unable to bear it any longer, he tried to put her on her back so he could shove it deep into her cunt.

She pushed firmly at his chest, saying, "No. This is *my* fuck. You just lie still and take it."

Amused by her arrogant tone of assumed domination, he obediently laid back, waited while she threw one leg over him and seated herself in place, his cock snugged up tight.

She had done this with Hale, occasionally but rarely, in the first days of marriage. However, with Hale's unimaginative love-making, the impulse to experiment had long since faded. Now she felt her breath catch in her body as slowly, slowly, savoring the length of his cock, its immediately responsive pulsation, she rocked up and down, feeling it deeper than she had ever felt even *this* great cock.

On an impulse, she leaned forward to grasp both his wrists, raising his arms over his head and pinning them there. Braced so, holding him down, she began fucking with rapid swings of her hips, as fast and undulant as a hula dancer, until he gasped delightfully under the thrust of her hot pussy.

When, his breath caught short, he began to struggle, she thought he was putting it on for her benefit. Then, somehow, she caught the whiff of panic, heard echoing in her head the exultant thought: *He's terrified by the idea of being helpless, he hates and loves being pinned down*, and she fucked him in greater abandonment and mastery than ever.

His body strained against her as he struggled to free his arms. Exultantly conquering, she gripped his wrists all the more firmly. He gasped in panic . . . he had turned pale. Through clenched teeth, he said, low but urgent, "Let me up. Let me *up*, damn it!"

In the same instant, he felt himself swept up into a gale

of lust, his spine melting in an orgasm more powerful than he had ever felt. He yielded himself helplessly even as he fought her, he was coming, coming, *God, what a great coming* . . .

Her voice snapped at him like a whip. "Don't come, damn you! Don't you *dare* come yet!"

He opened his eyes, to stare up into her face. He had never seen a woman look as she did now, so fierce and demanding that her face was almost ugly, and utterly beautiful, as she bucked and twisted on him, compelling him to obey the command of her writhing flesh.

She said through clenched teeth, "Now, damn it, *now!*" releasing him into orgasm, his ejaculation pulsing into her own terrific orgasm, not once but twice and three times, as together they mounted higher and higher, finally to slide satisfied down the other side of the mountain.

She released him and lay down on his body, her pussy writhing slowly against his limp cock. It startled him when she put her sucking mouth on his nipple. He wanted to flinch away but it was good, so good that his body trembled and flinched in sensuous weakness.

She lay upon his conquered flesh, feeling her own flesh conquered also. His warm cock lay limply in the slit of her pussy, feeling good there, sweet and undemanding. She breathed deeply, with satisfaction. A part of her being, that had never been called on, had been brought forth in this great fucking, so far beyond the thousands of beautifully fulfilling fantasies she had shaped in her mind.

Finally, with a great sigh, she disengaged herself to sit beside his prone body. She stroked her palm across his chest, sensitive to the texture of matted hair.

"I have never fucked a man like that," she said in honest gratefulness. "Thank you."

"I've never been fucked like that by a woman." He smiled. "So why are you thanking *me?*"

"I felt a way I've never felt before," she said, exploring what had happened inside her. "I think *every* woman needs to feel like that sometimes, but the man never gives her a chance . . ." Her eyes shifted to his face. "You liked it, didn't you, being held down like that . . . ?"

"I hated it," he said. "But, God, did it turn me on!"

"You see, something in a man must need that style of fucking, too, at times." She frowned. "A man is partly a woman, just as a woman is partly a man. After all, we get genes from both parents, the male and the female. We just . . . most of the time, we refuse to recognize it in ourselves, as though such recognition would destroy our basic maleness . . . or femaleness."

"Some people go in for bondage, all that business," he said dubiously. "I guess it's all a part of it, masochism . . ."

"I don't like those big scientific words, I just . . . like the way I felt. I wouldn't want to have it like that *all* the time." She was looking at him again. "But can I have it like that again if I want it?"

"Sure," he said. "Of course." Underneath, he was uneasy with the assurance. He had been truly desperate to escape there for a minute, until he had surrendered to the incredible orgasm.

She stirred. "Well. I don't think we can top that, do you?" She laughed. "Besides, I've still got my grocery shopping to do."

He glanced at his watch. "Yes. It's time." His voice was quiet, fulfilled.

She leaned forward to kiss him, her hand reaching the length of his body to trail tantalizing fingers across his crotch. "You beautiful man," she said, crooning as she had crooned over his cock. "The most beautiful man in the world. And mine, all mine."

He lay without lifting his arms, letting her have him entirely. "Beautiful woman," he whispered.

"I love you, I lust for you," she crooned, "I've never had it all before, love and lust and all."

He looked into her dear face, feeling closer than he had ever felt with anyone. Even Eleanor. He could, for the first time in his life, say the thing he had never dared think about.

"The next time," he said. He had to strengthen his voice. "There's something *I've* done a thousand times in my imagination, but . . ."

"Anything," she whispered. "I'm all yours, like you're all mine. There isn't anything I won't do with you." She brought her hand up to trace his mouth with a fingertip. "This time was mine; you gave it to me after I gave you my mouth. Next time, it's your turn."

He stirred restlessly, unable to say it. "Just think about it, that's all. You don't have to promise, just promise to think about it."

"I'll think about it," she whispered. "Tell me."

"I've never . . . I've always wanted to fuck a woman in the . . . in the . . ." He couldn't say it. "In the *other* place."

Her teeth bit into her lower lip; not in the revulsion he had expected, only in puzzlement. "What do you . . . oh!" She regarded him doubtfully. "Can it be *done?*"

"Of course. It's how homosexuals do it, some of them anyway. So of course a man and a woman can, too." He paused. Hastily he added, "I've never fantasied it with a man, of course. But with a woman . . ."

"I should think it would hurt terribly," she said, still doubtful.

"Just think about it, that's all," he urged.

She smiled. "Of course I'll think about it. I'll even *try,* but . . ." She shivered. "But I won't promise."

"We'll try it together, very easy, very gentle," he promised. Overwhelmed with affection for her willingness, he held her close as he whispered, "We'll have everything, won't we? All there is, all the different ways."

She yielded, but only momentarily. "I have got to get out of here!"

Awkward in the space, so much more confining now that the love-making was over, they got dressed more or less simultaneously. She slid over the front seat behind the wheel, but he had to get out to replace the bicycle. It did not occur to either of them that he could ride the bike just as well from here; they were less than a mile from the rendezvous point.

"Hey, it's stopped raining," he called from outside.

She cranked down the misted window. The rain was definitely over, though there were still clouds. A fresh smell rose from the earth, the air was washed clean. As, she thought, so much is washed clean between us. Now that we have yielded ourselves to each other, everything is clean and simple and beautiful. We must always keep it that way.

"I just hope you don't get rained on before you get home," she said anxiously as he got in beside her. She put her hand on his thigh. "Your shorts are still pretty damp."

"I'm all warm inside," he said, laughing.

She backed the car out of the grove and drove quickly to the place where they had first met—it always seems *right* to part at this exact spot, she thought, though why I shouldn't take him nearer home, especially with the threat of rain, I don't know.

He put a hand to the door handle. "I guess it's good-bye again until Next Thursday." He sighed quietly. "It always seems like such a long time, one Thursday to the next."

"Wait a minute," she said rapidly. "There's just one thing."

He took his hand away. "Yes?" Surprise, apprehension, in his voice.

She found it hard to say. "Just one thing," she repeated, unable to look at him. "We can't be like those other people." She looked at him. "We won't be, will we?"

"What do you mean?"

"I mean: We've got to keep it secret. It's our own special thing, our little world, like in the station wagon this afternoon behind the curtain of rain . . ."

His voice was patient. "I don't think I understand."

She was stronger with it now. "I mean, we can't start seeing each other except during our time together. We've never known each other socially." She looked at him pleadingly. "Let's keep it that way."

He was genuinely puzzled; he could not follow her thinking. "Well, sure, I don't see why we should."

Her voice was urgent. "We *shouldn't,* that's what I mean. I don't want us to be at parties together, aware of each other all the time like those other people are. I couldn't stand being in a room with you in some friend's house, thinking, *I fuck that man;* or knowing that you're standing over there with a drink in your hand, thinking about having fucked me. Do you understand?"

"Yes. You want to keep it *ours.*"

Her voice was fierce; her hand pounded the steering wheel. "Yes. Yes. It's a separate life we've got, it has nothing to do with your wife or my husband, your children or my children, your friends or my friends."

She stopped, began again. "I don't even want us to get in the habit of calling each other unless it's a dire necessity. I don't want to hear about what you did with your time away from me, or tell you what I did with mine."

"All right," he said quietly. "If that's the way you want it, that's how it will be."

"That's how it *has* to be." Then, slowly, she added, "I don't want to go to your cabin again, either. We'll find a motel somewhere, *private,* like it was private today in the station wagon, in the rain."

"A motel would be more difficult," he pointed out. "Riskier."

"I don't care," she said rapidly. "I know, in the beginning I said I *couldn't* go to a motel with you. But it's better. In a motel, we'll be in a bed where you haven't made love with your wife, maybe fucked other women . . ."

"Now, don't start that," he protested. "You're the first and only . . ."

"All right, all right," she said impatiently. She could feel the tears in her eyes waiting to reveal themselves; not from sorrow, anger, but from the impossibility of making his male mind understand how she felt. She could hear the whimper in her voice. "You must give me this, darling. Because I have to have it."

"*All right!*" he said in exasperation. Then, his hand folding warmly over hers, he smiled forgivingly. "Our love

108

will belong to us, with the rest of the world all the way outside."

She put her wet cheek against the back of his hand. "Thank you. Thank you." She straightened. "You'll have to arrange about the motel room, then call me Thursday morning—exactly between ten and ten-thirty, no other time—and tell me where it is, so we can meet in the room."

He was always nonplussed by her sudden return out of whatever emotion—tenderness, lust, even anger—to a direct and immediate practicality. But he had to point out the contradiction.

"I thought we decided not to call each other."

"I meant simply for a moment's conversation," she said placidly. "This is necessary."

"We could meet here, like we've always done," he argued. "Go together to the motel . . ."

She shook her head. "It's silly, having to ride your bicycle regardless of the weather." She made her voice firm. "No. You drive there, I drive there, we're together only in the room. Actually, it'll be much safer."

"All right," he said in resignation. "Fine with me."

She faced him. "You do know it's because I love you so very much." Her voice was tender again. "It's so real, so true . . . we can't be just fucking around like all those other people."

He found it necessary to deflect her intensity. "You know, you say that, now—'fucking,' I mean—without having to grit your teeth to get the word out like you used to do."

Used to do, he thought irrelevantly, as though we've been together for years.

Her voice was quiet. "I can even, in my mind, call your cock a cock instead of that silly name I've always used. Because, darling, you have made me free. Free to lust, like I'm free to love. *Free to fuck your cock.*"

He laughed and kissed her, feeling a swift stroke of happiness. She gave him so much. She gave him everything. His hand wanted to touch her breast, but she said, "Go, now. Our time is up."

He took the full meaning of what time together meant to her, how hard she was fighting to keep it separate from all else in their lives. It was, after all, how he wanted it, too. Had to have it.

He grinned at her. "You were something today," he said tenderly.

She grinned at him. "I'm always something," she said. "Next week, I'll be something else."

He had to whisper it. "Think about it. Make it something you *want* me to do."

She whispered also. "Yes. I already am."

The Woman:

She had always enjoyed being alone in the house most of every day. These days, so empty without *him*, however, she found herself restless. It was not enough to make the usual milk runs to grocery store and dry cleaner, following the basic routines of a middle-class life.

She found herself, instead, visiting areas of the city she had never known: the bus station, an arcade of fancy video games infested by teen-agers, the sleazy downtown streets. She stood across the street from the bank where *he* worked, gazing up, wondering which window was his.

For a full minute she believed she had the nerve to walk in and ask for an appointment, just to view him in his workaday world. She could, after all, be applying for a loan on a new car; many married women nowadays made their own financial transactions. But, knowing such an intrusion would be in violation of her own laid-down rules, she did not enter.

Soon, she knew that she was watching people; something inside her needed to know more than she had ever allowed herself to understand about how other people lived their private lives. People-watching, she discovered, is a fascinating hobby. In love herself, sexually attracted and sexually attractive, she was sensitive to the half-secret desires and dreams of strangers.

She watched a shabby, middle-aged man follow a young woman for blocks, admiring the seductive movement of her ass in a tight pair of fashionable jeans. The girl, without looking around, betrayed her subliminal awareness by a subtle enhancement of body movement, a certain tilt to her head, her glance secretly admiring her image in the shop windows.

When she turned to cross the street, she looked, with excessive casualness, to assess her admirer. The haughty toss of the girl's head as she rejected him in one glance was so comic that she burst out laughing, startling a passerby. The middle-aged man, sensing and accepting the rejection, followed no more. Retracing half a block, he hesitated yearningly before an establishment with discreetly blacked-out windows before entering.

That was how she discovered the sex shop. She gazed thoughtfully at the revealing legend—"ADULT SHOP" —before proceeding on her random way.

Tiring finally of walking, she entered the bus station, where she could sit down. As she rested, she watched the flow of travelers. A sailor made a bold approach to a girl who looked too young—couldn't be more than fourteen—to be available for such sexual games. She laughed at whatever words the sailor had used for an opening and quickly they were chattering away, the slender boy in his sailor suit so appealing, with sexual tension apparent in every move, that it made an ache in her heart for all the sailor boys she had never had.

She smiled to herself, thinking that, before her lover had entered her life, she might well have incorporated this youthful fire and vigor into a sexual daydream.

Her mind shifted abruptly to the Adult Shop. Its stock-in-trade, of course, would be "adult" books and magazines —what used to be called *dirty* books and magazines—and sexual apparatus of various kinds. Her education in such matters extended only to a *Playboy* that the girls in her high school class had passed giggling among themselves one spring until it had become tattered. To her youthful eyes, even then, the vaunted centerfold, the air-brushed "Varga Girls," had seemed quite innocent.

She had heard there were now magazines for women that showed naked pictures of men. Pictures of *naked* men, she corrected, absent-minded in her reverie. She wondered if it would excite her to gaze upon a photograph of a man's sexual apparatus. It seemed to excite men to see a beautiful woman naked. She didn't believe a mere picture, no matter how provocative, could insinuate itself into her sexual daydreams. She had never been one to imagine erotic encounters with movie stars or professional athletes.

She would, at the least, learn something from such revealment. She had, after all, been acquainted with —*intimately associated with*, she corrected with a mental giggle—only three cocks in her life. Billy-Bob. Hale. *Him*. So, she reflected, I really have no standards of comparison.

I was terrified by the sight of Billy-Bob's cock. I'm so familiar with Hale's, I'm comfortable with it, I know exactly what to expect and, more importantly, what *not* to expect (and fond of it, too, after all Hale's cock gave me my daughters). I am terribly excited by *his* beautiful cock, the only one I've tasted in my mouth.

In a warm rush of forgotten memory, she recalled where and when she had acquired the designation "bird." She had been only eight, playing with the nine-year-old boy who had just moved in down the street.

He had told her, with an air of great mystery, that he'd show her his "bird" if she would sneak with him into his garage.

Thinking of an exotic bird well worth the seeing— perhaps even a gaudy talking parrot—she followed eagerly. Inside the garage, however, he had exhibited his cock instead, standing tiny and stiff through the fly of his plaid shorts.

She gazed at it with a puzzled frown. "Where's the *bird* you promised to show me?"

"You're looking at my bird," he said, giggling. "And *you've* got the nest where it lights."

"What *are* you talking about?"

"Stand still, and I'll show you."

Obedient to her own curiosity, she submitted to his hands pushing her shorts and underpants down to her ankles.

"See? My bird goes right into your nest, and then it lays an egg," he said, giggling again. "That's how you get babies, didn't you know that? Lie down, and I'll show you."

Not sure she wanted a baby, she refused to lie down. But

she did want to see an egg come out of his bird, so she allowed him to demonstrate standing up.

To her astonishment, his stiff little bird fitted neatly inside her nest. She stood with legs apart, braced against the car fender, while he squirmed it in and out. She kept watching for the egg, but it never came, and when she got tired of waiting she simply pulled away.

It *had* felt nice—sort of like when she touched herself there—but she forgot the episode promptly and the next Saturday, when the boy suggested eagerly that he put his bird into her nest again, she pretended she didn't know what he was talking about.

She had, she reflected now, suppressed all memory of the incident, leaving her mind as virgin as her body. The only trace remaining was the silly names for sexual organs, when she had grown up enough to need such names.

At the vivid remembrance, her nest had warmed—which brought her to an abrupt discovery. She had now accepted "cock"—even gloried in it. But she thought still of her "nest."

Why should that be? She had fully intended to bring the forbidden word to a mental speaking. But something in her mind resisted "pussy" or "cunt," even "vagina." Because they're names given to the female organ by the males of the species, she decided. Those male names always have about them something dirty and demeaning.

In this moment of honesty, she realized another new thing, more startling because it was *now*. She was dwelling on these self-forgotten thoughts and deeds to keep herself from entertaining the knowledge that she was tempted powerfully to explore the Adult Shop.

Yes. Seriously. Perhaps buy one of those magazines designed for the titillation of womankind, smuggle it home to pore secretly over its secrets. The idea horrified her. The place would surely be full of dirty old men leering at her female presence, maybe even groping her, making indecent suggestions . . .

Such a thing was unlike her. Yet, while the upper part of her mind flinched coyly from the impossibility, a cooler part of her mind whispered: If magazines for women are on sale, surely they expect women customers to come in and buy.

There was also, she told herself, the mystery of sex paraphernalia, in which she was utterly ignorant. *He* had said something, last Thursday, about bondage. She didn't know what gear was involved—ropes, belts, handcuffs? She only knew that when she had held him down he had resisted violently, finally to submit with a peculiarly intense passion. And she . . . She had felt . . .

Remembering, she was more aroused than by the memory of her first tiny nine-year-old bird. Lust gave her courage; telling herself she could walk into the shop like everybody else, she started resolutely out of the bus station.

The sailor and the girl, she noted, were playing a Pac-Man machine. He stood behind her, crotch pressing against her, as he instructed her in strategy. When he shifted she saw, clearly defined in the tight pants, the hard-on he was rubbing surreptitiously against her. The girl's buttocks were arched backward, acknowledging the erection, welcoming it.

It made her warmer still, and she found herself hurrying. But, her courage ebbing, she thought, What if somebody I know is in there? So embarrassing to run into Paul, or Harry, or . . . Even Rosemary; the hated Rosemary was quite capable of any such outrageous notion.

Averting her face, she continued past the blacked-out windows. Ashamed of her cowardice, she marched helplessly to the station wagon, got behind the wheel, and drove home.

The temptation did not go away. Not enough to have a clandestine lover . . . though that was indeed a great change from the woman she had been only three weeks ago. She had discovered a brand-new world in which she was like a child. Surely she should have the courage to explore it.

After all, she intended to allow *him* to have his strange way Next Thursday—didn't she?, doubtful as she was. Only last night, tentatively, she had touched herself *there*. So tight and small, she didn't see how his great cock could enter that untried hole. But if he wants to try, she had told herself bravely . . . and she knew, didn't she, that he meant to try?

That, also, would take courage; the same kind of courage that had deserted her today.

Somewhere that night between not sleeping and sleeping, she knew that tomorrow she would make herself enter the Adult Shop. She would see all that was there to be seen.

During the morning, not letting herself think about her plan, she kept busy with meaningless tasks. She cleaned the stove unnecessarily, she took everything out of the refrigerator and wiped the shelves with baking soda. She took too much time folding the washing, remembering that she still had the sheets from the cabin, washed and dried and secretly stowed away; and what in the world would she do with them, now that they weren't going to the cabin ever again?

Despite the delaying tactics, she knew she meant to carry out her mission of sex education. Somewhere inside her mind, she had stepped over a line and now she couldn't *not* go.

She dressed differently from her usual mode, finding in her closet an old navy-blue linen suit she hadn't worn for years. She put on her most sensible pair of shoes, and the floppy-brimmed hat she had bought for a cousin's wedding. She surveyed herself in the glass, satisfied that no one who knew her could possibly recognize her without a close look.

She parked the station wagon two blocks away. Approaching from the opposite side of the shabby street, she stood watching from a doorway, where she was ostensibly inspecting cut-rate shoes.

Two men entered, a third departed. He walked quickly away, she noted in trembly amusement, after a furtive glance up and down the sidewalk. She wasn't the only one who didn't wish to be seen patronizing the place. Finally, to her relief, she saw a woman push open the door and disappear inside.

All right, she told herself. That's the signal you've been waiting for. It's now or never. As excited as if she were going to meet her lover, she walked down to the traffic light, crossed, walked up the other side.

Not allowing herself pause, she pushed open the door and went in. She didn't stop there, either, but kept her legs moving, not looking at anyone she passed, until she had reached the back of the small room. Half-hidden behind a rack of books, heart thumping with her own boldness, she surveyed the scene.

The store was smaller than she had expected. There was a counter near the entrance, an old man on a stool behind it. Three lines of book racks; the otherwise-bare walls displayed erotic calendars. Along the near side was a series of glass-topped display cases. She wanted to look into them, but did not yet dare.

Several men were browsing along the book racks. The woman who had entered ahead of her was in another corner of the room, head down, examining a book. A new customer, a man, entered and walked briskly down the length of the room. To her surprise, he disappeared through a back door.

She gazed at the sign over that door: "GARDEN OF DELIGHT MASSAGE PARLOR. MEN ONLY." So it's not only books and gadgets, she thought with a secret thrill. There's *that* upstairs, too.

She didn't know about massage parlors, either. She held a vague notion that it was a matter of pretty young girls giving men erotic massages, maybe even masturbating them, but not actually having sex. Perhaps they *do* them like I did *him*, she decided, and then: How would it be to *do* one strange man after another? You'd have to really like the taste of a man's cock. Or maybe it's simply for money, just as women will be prostitutes, or wait on tables topless or bottomless.

She was drawn to the display cases. Slowly she moved in that direction, surveying the racks of books as she passed.

Thin books, cheaply made, with outrageous titles. She was astonished at the prices.

The first display case showed a black-rubber suit, remarkably like a scuba-diving outfit, laid out flat in the case. It was illustrated in action by a poster of an exotic blonde dressed in the same outfit, skin tight, her breasts bulging impossibly, her crotch deeply outlined. She stood with feet braced on very high heels, brandishing a whip. There was, she noted, a whip supplied with the outfit.

That's one thing for sure I wouldn't care for, she told herself firmly, passing on to the next case. I've never had any problem whatsoever distinguishing between pain and pleasure. It must be a male thing.

The next case displayed dildoes of various sizes, some enormous, made of ivory or plastic. Among them she saw something labeled "Ben-Wa balls," luxuriantly nestled, like a pair of cufflinks or earrings, in a plush jeweler's box.

She stared at the Ben-Wa balls, trying to figure out their use. It'd have to be that a woman would insert them in her . . . in her pussy. Maybe somehow they masturbated a woman, like the dildoes. Except, it'd have to be by their own action. A booklet accompanied the set; but of course she'd have to buy the balls to read the booklet. They seemed to be Japanese; the Japanese, she had always heard, were supposed to be clever and sophisticated about sex.

She looked around again. She could buy the Ben-Wa balls if she wanted to, couldn't she? But what if they got *lost* up there? It would be necessary to go to her doctor. She had read about gynecologists having to take strange objects out of women's vaginas. She felt herself shrivel with the shame she would feel, going to old gray-haired Dr. Plummer for such a purpose.

The next case showed belts and ropes and, yes, flimsy handcuffs. This poster displayed a black-haired woman, naked, head bowed, hands crossed and tied in front of her. So this was the bondage *he* had talked about. What if she had actually tied his hands with a rope—ankles tied, too —he'd have gone really crazy then. She had only held

118

down his wrists with her hands and the weight of her upper body, and it had driven him wild.

She wondered apprehensively if she would be allowed to leave without buying something. Maybe, otherwise, they wouldn't let a person look over the merchandise. Though certainly everybody in the room was browsing away at a great rate. As she watched, a man put down the magazine he was looking at and disappeared behind the secret door at the back of the room. Had to get up his courage, as well as his cock, to go up there, she thought understandingly.

Maybe she'd buy a *Playgirl*, except she hadn't yet found the magazines for women. The woman was still in the far corner; that must be where they were displayed.

Not wanting to get too near the old man at the cash register, she crossed the back of the room. Copies of *Playboy, Chic, Hustler;* she had no desire to look at naked women, she *knew* about women from her own body.

As she rounded the back corner of the long wooden rack, the woman customer, without looking up, moved away. She was intensely grateful that no one in this place seemed to look at anyone else. She was still experiencing the faint sense of shame with which she had entered.

She found it suddenly extraordinary that a business selling sex objects could flourish in the city—so staid and old-fashioned in so many ways—she had grown up in. There were high-school bands marching in parades, football games, the American Legion and the Elks and the Rotary. There were garden clubs for the women, the Y for the kids, and more churches than you'd think a city this size could support. Yet . . . here was also the Adult Shop with an upstairs massage parlor, the Garden of Delight.

And here *I* am, browsing like everybody else, she thought, mentally shaking her head. She saw, then, the magazines for women; her hand was reaching to pick up a copy of *Playgirl*.

She was disappointed to discover that, because it was heatsealed in plastic, she would have to buy it without scanning the contents. It didn't seem fair. A flicker of familiar movement caught her eye. She looked up just in

119

time to see the back of a man disappearing through the doorway leading upstairs.

Her breath locked in her body. *She was sure it had been Hale.*

Instantaneously her mind, her body, her entire being rejected the idea. It couldn't possibly have been Hale, so dear, so familiar, so *known*. Yet . . . the very familiarity of movement and posture had caught the corner of her eye.

Desperately she told herself, I had only a glimpse. All I saw, really, was his back. Some stranger, surely, who happens to resemble Hale superficially, seen from behind like that.

Her hands were trembling, her whole body. She told herself, Get out, I've got no business here anyhow, *why did I ever come?* But, as she commanded her body toward escape, she realized that she could not leave without *knowing*.

There was a part of her that did not want to know; the part that remained convinced it *had* been Hale, after all. And if it is him? she thought miserably. *What then?*

She made herself pay attention to the erotic materials, displayed so enticingly, in an effort to submerge herself in the atmosphere. She kept her head down, shadowing her face under the brim of the hat, her eyes flickering constantly toward that secret doorway. How long did they stay up there, anyway?

The first man she had seen enter, the one moving so purposefully and unashamed, emerged as she looked. Not fifteen minutes since he had gone up. Somehow it made her feel better, as though the greater evils could not possibly be accomplished in such a brief time.

I'll just wait, see that it is a stranger, not Hale after all, she told herself. Then I won't be accusing him in my mind of something he would never, ever, do. Why, Hale *loved* her, always had, he had married her, even after Billy-Bob, for she had been the only woman for him.

Billy-Bob, she remembered suddenly, had joined the Marines after failing to make first string in college football. Hale had got drunk the night they had heard about their old high-school classmate being killed in Vietnam. She had been surprised, she remembered, to learn that Billy-Bob's real name had been William Robert Radley.

She was no longer trembling, but cold as stone. She kept looking blindly at the *Playgirl* in her hands, turning it over, turning it over again, reading the provocative titles on the front cover, "The Weekend Marriage," "Sex in Public Places."

It was Hale.

She saw him emerge hurrying through the door; he didn't want to look at anybody, see anybody looking at him. Frozen into a mental catalepsy, she studied him intently from under the brim of her hat. That expression on his face showed him to be so much more satisfied than all her wifely love, all her passion, had ever made him.

She watched him walk through the store and vanish into the street. He was wearing his nice gray suit, too, that she had always liked so much. She had picked out that suit for him, had chosen the silver-and-gray-banded tie to go with it.

She wanted desperately to depart from this terrible place. But she knew she could not leave until Hale had got out of the vicinity. She waited for what seemed an interminable time before she could start moving toward the door.

She walked blindly, her legs stiff as the legs of a robot. She was numb, mentally and physically, she would never feel sensation, emotion, again. She fumbled at the outside door, heard the old man say from behind the cash register: "You gonna pay for that magazine before you leave, lady?"

She turned, fumbled in her purse for money, pushed a bill at him. He rang up the sale as though it were a box of aspirin, and slipped the magazine into a plain brown paper bag. Then she was outside, clutching the bag, clutching her still-open purse, clutching her change.

The next thing was, go to the station wagon. She began walking, moving as though she had to learn all over again how to put one foot in front of the other. She had read somewhere that walking was simply a controlled falling.

How had the first half-human to stand upright learned to control his falling? She felt with each step as though she were falling.

She reached the station wagon. She had to unlock it before she could get in. To unlock it, she had to find the keys. Oh God, it was impossible to find the keys and to unlock the door and to get inside, where she would be safe.

Somehow she found the keys, held her shaking hand still long enough to insert the proper key, and it worked as it was supposed to work. Only inside the car did she collapse, her body crumpling over the wheel as her mind had already crumpled under the confirmation of Hale, yes, really and truly Hale, going upstairs into the Garden of Delight to get his cock sucked by some woman. She wanted to cry. She had thought she was going to cry. But the grief in her was a grief beyond tears.

She had to go somewhere. But there was nowhere to go. She could not return home, not yet, maybe not ever; Hale, *her husband*, would be too much present in the house in which they had lived for most of their marriage.

She started the engine. Because the engine was running, she had to pull away from the curb. Driving aimlessly, she was in the heart of downtown before she realized it wasn't aimless after all. She stared across the street at the bank building. I have to talk to *him*, she thought. *Now*.

It was in violation of all that was between them. She couldn't help that. She must walk in, tell his secretary she had an appointment, talk to him privately in his private office. Surely, once he knew, he would understand why it had to be.

She got out of the station wagon, walked across with the light, turned up the street. Through the wide glass window she could see the people inside; tellers in their cages, customers standing in line. What if he doesn't have a private office? she thought. Many bank officers work in a sort of bullpen, right on the floor with the customers, and even if he is a vice-president . . .

She kept on walking. On the corner, she saw a telephone

kiosk, offering deliverance. She would call him, he would come out to meet her.

The telephone book had been vandalized, leaving only the safety chain dangling. She proceeded on up the street. Only in the third block did she find a kiosk with a tattered directory still in place.

She found the bank number. I'll have to be brisk and self-assured, she warned herself. Matter-of-fact. The switchboard answered, next his secretary; then she heard *his* voice saying, "Hello. Can I help you?"

"It's me," she whispered, gripping the telephone tightly.

She heard the instant apprehension. "What's the matter?"

"I've got to talk to you," she whispered. "Now."

"Where are you?"

"Three blocks up the street."

"I saw you." It sounded like an accusation. "I happened to be looking out the window. I wouldn't have recognized you if it hadn't been for the station wagon. It didn't occur to me, however, that . . ."

"I meant to come into the bank, but decided it would be better . . ." Her voice faltered. "Can you come out to meet me?"

"Now?" he said in alarm. "Right *now*?"

"I have to talk to you," she repeated, her knuckles gripping the telephone so hard they turned white.

His voice was hurried. "I've got a board meeting in five minutes. No way I can get out of a board meeting."

"You have to," she said urgently, though she knew by now it was no use.

His words were rapid, unassailable. "Listen, go on home. As soon as the board meeting is over, I'll call you there. All right?"

"All right," she said hopelessly and hung up before he did. He only wanted to get her out of the downtown area, *anywhere*, as long as she wasn't threatening to visit him in his place of business.

She drove home, concentrating hard, as if she had had a few drinks too many, telling herself this was no time for an accident. She had never had an accident, she was always a careful driver.

The house loomed threatening, when always it had been a sanctuary. *There are no more sanctuaries,* she thought, letting herself in from the carport through the kitchen. All the sanctuaries have been destroyed. Simply because I wanted so strongly to *know.*

She sat down in the living room, looked about her as though it were the house of a stranger. It *was* a stranger's house, though this was where she lived; she, and Hale, and the twins. Except Hale hasn't *been* here, she thought. All along, he's been living his secret life. As I've been living *my* secret life, first in fantasy, then in reality.

An hour passed, in which she did nothing, before the telephone rang. She decided not to answer, but it rang so insistently that finally she was forced to pick it up.

"Thank goodness. I was afraid you hadn't got home yet," he said, his voice tiny in her ear.

She listened to the now-familiar timbre of his voice, discovering that the sound of it, so distant and so irrelevant, left her cold.

"Yes," she said. "I'm here."

"What's happened?"

She thought: He's afraid Hale has found out. That's his total concern.

"Nothing, really," she said. "I just got upset. I'm all right now."

His voice probed. "Are you sure?"

"Yes," she said. "I just want to go lie down for a while. Thank you for calling."

Surely he could hear the distance in her tone, for he said anxiously, "You *are* going to be there Thursday, aren't you?"

"Yes," she said impatiently. "Of course."

He sounded relieved. "OK, I'll talk to you Thursday morning."

"You do that," she said. She waited to see if he would hang up. He did, so she hung up also.

She should have been busy in the kitchen when Hale got home. Instead, empty inside herself, she was still lying on the bed.

Hale came into the room, saying in mild surprise, "Well, hello, so here you are."

She had fully intended to confront him with her discovery. Now, she realized, it was impossible. How could she explain why she had been in the Adult Shop in the first place?

"Let's eat out," she said in a dulled voice, sitting up. "I don't feel like cooking today."

"Got a load of work in my briefcase," Hale said dubiously. He never liked eating out, just the two of them.

She began taking off her blouse; she was still wearing the outfit she had chosen for the expedition and somehow it felt dirty on her body.

"We haven't eaten out since the girls went off to camp," she said sharply. "Unless you count the cookout last week. I get tired of cooking two meals a day, every day."

"All right," he assented unhappily. "Let's eat out."

She went past him, still not looking at him, to finish undressing in the bathroom. She did not take time for the soaking bath she wanted so badly, only a quick shower. When she came out, wrapped in a protective bathrobe, he had gone out of the bedroom. She hastened to dress before he returned.

Only from across the table at Maury's Chophouse could she make herself look at him. He sat facing her, so near, once so dear—still so familiar. Worry showed in his eyes; though he couldn't know why, he sensed that she was upset, annoyed . . . perhaps angry.

"So you didn't have a very good day of it," he said, showing a tentative smile.

"I didn't," she said shortly and gulped at her drink.

I wish I'd never knocked that man off his bicycle, never taken him for a lover, she thought fiercely. I could slam Hale with it then, hit him hard and walk out. Decide

125

afterward whether I want a divorce. But make him know what he's done to me.

Under the circumstances, she could do nothing. Besides, she thought guiltily, if it hadn't been for *him*, I'd never have been there. I could have lived the rest of my life without knowing what I know now.

"Ready to order?" Hale asked gently. "Or do you want another drink first?"

It was always Hale's instinct to walk softly around the edges of a quarrel, hoping it would go away without anybody having to do anything dramatic. It was of a piece with his practice of law, ever anxious to compromise. Hale had often said he felt defeated as an attorney when he had to take a case into court, because in court nobody really won.

In our twenty years together, we've never had a satisfactory quarrel, she thought soberly. *That* is a lot of what's wrong with our marriage.

The bitter thought startled her. She had not believed, even when she had taken her lover, that anything was seriously wrong with their family life. Maybe not the most exciting thing in the world, living with Hale. But the reasons, evident and obscure, for giving herself to another man had had, she had thought, nothing to do with her marriage.

The liquor bolstering her courage, she could watch Hale's face, his eyes, his hands, as she asked, "And how was *your* day?"

"Oh, the usual thing," he said offhandedly.

The casualness of the reply stung her. Was it the "usual thing" to go out during lunch hour and hire a woman to masturbate him? Or to put her mouth on his cock and get him off that way? Maybe even *fuck* him, she added doggedly, because *I* don't know what goes on up there. And how much does he pay her? Surely it must be worth it . . . Hale has never been one to waste money.

The rush of thoughts was trembling into reckless words; she had to bite her lip to keep them silent. The waiter came with the menus, interposing the welcome distraction of placing their orders. She chose the most expensive cut of meat—steak with rock lobster tails—thinking viciously, If he can afford to hire some girl to suck him off, he can afford to buy his wife the best meal on the menu.

She realized then, to her astonishment, the intense jealousy burning in her heart. Jealousy of that unknown woman who had today given her husband something *she* had failed, apparently for years, to give him.

But I was the perfect wife, she thought in agony. Hale always said so, our friends envied us. Until the past weeks, she had never *looked* at another man. While, obviously, today was not the first time Hale had visited the Garden of Delight; his very attitude, the bearing of his body, had betrayed that he was a habitual customer.

The food came. With the first bite of steak, she knew she could not eat. She was hungry, she hadn't had lunch today; but, though she chewed conscientiously, she couldn't choke it down. Discreetly she disposed of the mouthful into her napkin. She set her knife and fork down, saying ruefully, thinking about the cost, "I guess I'll have to take it home in a doggy bag."

Hale peered across the table, concerned. "Are you ill?"

"No," she snapped. "I'm not ill. I just don't feel well."

While she waited for Hale, her hunger made her try once, then again, to eat. She forced the lobster tails down, but little of the meat. When the waiter came to check the table, he asked with appropriate concern, "The steak was not to your liking, madame?"

"It was fine, I just wasn't very hungry," she said apologetically. "Will you put it in a doggy . . . ?" She smiled at him. "In a *people* bag?"

He chuckled dutifully and bore the plate away, returning with the meat in a white bag.

"Ready to go?" Hale asked.

"Let's have one more drink," she said. Anything to delay going home, getting into bed with him. She thought in sudden terror: What if he comes at me tonight with his cock hanging out, wanting sex?

I won't be able to bear it, she thought in despair. Then Hale will *know* I know something.

They were silent in the car, but they nearly always were, so that was all right. In the living room, Hale glanced ruefully at the briefcase, saying, "Well, I suppose it's too late to start on that."

"Go ahead if you like. I'll just tuck up in bed and read until I'm sleepy," she urged.

He shook his head and went into the bathroom. She thought fatefully: He's still got sex on his mind. Maybe every time he comes to me it's because he visited the massage parlor that day. The thought was like an icy knife in her loins.

She got into bed, lay waiting. Her legs ached with tension, knowing she would have to yield her body if he gave the signal. Hale emerged wearing both halves of his pajamas. She breathed a secret sigh of relief; it was followed by an instant stroke of resentment. *She* satisfies him, she told herself bitterly. After he's been to *her*, he doesn't need me.

Hale got into bed and pulled up the sheet, turning his back to her as he always did in preparation for immediate sleep, saying gently, "I hope you'll feel better in the morning." Soon, she heard only the sound of his discreet snore.

She lay rigid, staring at the darkened ceiling. Suddenly, out of bitter resentment, a daring thought flashed through her fevered mind. *What if I turned him on his back, put my face into his groin, sucked him off?* Like I sucked *him* off. Is *that* what he's wanted, all these years, that I've never given him? Is a woman's mouth so important to a man?

The thought segued unexpectedly into a yearning desire to taste Hale's cock. It would be smaller in her mouth, gentler, sweeter than *his* cock. Lingering over the temptation, she warned herself; she dared not reveal to Hale that she knew about such things. Not after all these years in which the act had never been performed between them.

She knew, in black despair, that her problem—the resentment, the desire, the jealousy, mingled inextricably —was more complicated, and more perilous, than she had yet admitted to herself. She had held separate a secret

128

fantasy-life. Hale, too, had kept his fantasy-secrets from her. They were, she knew instinctively, as important to him as hers had always been to her, and—how long ago she did not know—he had found an outlet that had nothing to do with her.

She felt sadness, even a tenderness. Not simply for herself, for Hale; for every human being moving through life as sexual strangers, even to those most dear. *Especially* to those most dear.

Her lover? She knew *him*, she realized, no better than she knew her husband. Two lives had touched tenuously, like two fragile soap bubbles floating iridescent in a dream of free will, melding inseparably into a momentary union, then floating on again, sealed away from each other by the tension of their tender surfaces. Separate. Alone.

"I love you, Hale," she said softly into the darkness.

The information did not disturb the even tenor of his snoring. She did not know whether or not he had heard.

Throughout the interminable day that was Wednesday, she remained of two minds whether to see her lover tomorrow afternoon. At times it felt impossible *not* to meet him; other times, it was equally impossible to do so. He had been, after all—she kept reminding herself with whatever bitterness she could muster beyond the bitterness she felt toward Hale—a total wipe-out as far as providing the love and reassurance she had needed so desperately.

Yet, knowing of Hale's secret sex life, she was justified, wasn't she, in seeking her lover? In a momentary glow of euphoria, she dwelt warmly on the wonderful fucking last week in the back of the station wagon, isolated behind a curtain of rain that had misted the windows so opaquely they were hidden from all the world . . .

And before, when she had tasted his cock; had dared to make him come with her mouth; had drunk greedily of his oyster-come. It had satisfied *him* so thoroughly. Then, with bitterness: As thoroughly, no doubt, as that whore-woman satisfied Hale.

She had tried, without success, to imagine the scene in

the Garden of Delight. She didn't know what a massage parlor looked like; much less was she able to visualize Hale actually taking off his pants and his shorts and the necktie she had chosen to go with the gray suit, then letting the girl —she'd have to be young, she'd have to be reasonably good-looking, to work in a place like that—do it to him. *Pay* her to do it to him.

There ought to be massage parlors for us, too, she thought resentfully, where a woman can buy the same lustful ministrations from handsome young men. The attendants would be naked, of course—maybe not with erections, because of course to them it was only a job—but their hands rubbing, rubbing . . . their mouths on your pussy, as *his* mouth had been on her pussy. Then simply pay the money, as a man pays money to a woman, and take your satisfied leave.

For all she knew, in larger cities, there *were* places like that. She had read about the discos where women flocked by the hundreds to watch beautiful young men dance. There were the sex magazines for women, too; and only then did she remember the *Playgirl* she had bought.

Though she couldn't remember putting the magazine there, it was hidden on the shelf in her closet, still in the plain brown bag. She leafed through quickly, absorbing the shock of the photographs. Then, more slowly, she began to read.

Even the ads, for contraceptives and sex aids and substances guaranteeing to enlarge one's breasts, were beyond her previous ken. And the article on how to enjoy sexual titillation in public places—not the idea, so much, but the *tone* in which the article had been written, so archly aggressive, revealed a slant of female mind she wouldn't have believed possible. Indeed, she told herself, women *don't* think like that, so direct and dirty-minded. It's written to be a sexual come-on.

Toward the back, she discovered an article on sleeping with a male prostitute. Given her recent daydream of doing just that, she read it with avid curiosity. Only afterward did she discover that she had paid full price for a February copy, six months out of date.

Well, sex is certainly not topical, she thought philosophically as she leafed through one more time to gaze again upon the naked men. Their equipment is nothing to brag about, she couldn't help thinking; not nearly as impressive as her lover's cock. She had meant to bury the magazine in the garbage can. Instead, she replaced it carefully under a hatbox on the top shelf in her closet.

When the phone call came, she listened reluctantly —thinking about Hale, how, last night, she had known Hale sexually for the first time since the massage parlor —while *he* told her where the motel was located, the room number, how to get there.

"OK?" he said finally.

She had to say: "I don't think I can make it today."

It shook him. "What?" he said explosively. "After I've . . ."

"I'm not sure I *want* to make it." She searched for a reason to hide the real reason. "I'm not . . . I haven't felt like thinking about what you wanted me to think about. So I'm not *ready*."

"Come on anyway," he said urgently. "We don't have to talk about *that*, if you'd rather not."

She searched her mind, found it empty of inspiration. "All right. I'll be there."

She could not tell him—she scarcely believed it herself —about the passion with which, last night, she had opened herself to her errant husband.

It had started as a suppressed lust to taste Hale's cock in her mouth. Knowing that the almost irresistible desire was triggered by jealousy—a ferocious desire to prove she could perform a thousand times better than his whore—did not in the least assuage her raging desire.

Not daring to risk the gambit for fear of self-betrayal, the lust of her mouth transmuted directly into her loins; it surprised her as much as it surprised Hale when she went into uncontrollable orgasm in the very thrust of entering.

131

Even after initial release of the sexual tension that had been building ever since discovering his secret vice, she ignored Hale's four-minute stride toward ejaculation, begging, "Don't come yet, don't lose it, not yet, not yet" —forcing Hale into a continued fucking for an intense half-hour of heedless orgasms until at last, gasping with fatigue, he lost it finally and forever.

Filled with shame for her lustful, vengeful jealousy, she let him escape into sleep. She even went to sleep herself, only to wake to find herself snugged tightly against Hale's buttocks, one hand over his hip holding his cock. Realizing in shame that Hale was awake also, only pretending to be still asleep so he wouldn't have to fuck her again, she rolled carefully away to leave him in peace.

Across the breakfast table, Hale regarded her in silent perplexity. He couldn't help knowing now that a sea change had taken place in her. She sat opposite him, dreading the first question, for she had only one answer—if Hale accused her, she could defend herself only by revealing her knowledge of *his* secret sin against their marriage. Not wanting to open that great breach between them, she gratefully accepted Hale's continued silence. She was even more grateful when he found a means to leave the house while she was in the bathroom.

She had known then that this Thursday, of all Thursdays, she could not keep rendezvous with her lover. Not so much for the risk, as for the fact that Hale's cock, in more ways than one, dwelled still in her tender flesh.

The Two:

After a scouting trip past the motel, she decided to leave the station wagon at the adjacent shopping center, safely anonymous among the many parked cars. Such automatic surreptitiousness made her angry. She had expected to feel exposed until she had reached the room; instead, she stepped boldly across the divider, walked across the nearly empty motel parking lot, and knocked on the door.

He was wearing slacks, a short-sleeved sport shirt, loafers. It was the first time she had seen him in anything but a T-shirt and bicycling shorts.

He had the television on. "Shut that damn thing off," she said.

He obeyed, turning to regard her warily. She had moved past his welcoming embrace, to sit on the double bed that was the main feature of the room. As it should be, he thought wryly. That's what we're here for, isn't it?

Without preamble, sitting with hands folded in her lap, she began to talk about her husband. He listened, wanting to move to her but knowing it was impossible, at this moment, to do so. Anything he did or said right now, he recognized shrewdly, would be wrong.

Finished with the recital of bare facts, she glared up at him. "Then—I had to make love with him last night. That's when I thought of the worst thing. He could give me syphilis or . . . What's the other one?"

"Gonorrhea," he said. "More popularly known as the clap."

"Syphilis or gonorrhea," she repeated. "Or both. Not just last night. Any time over the years he's been going there."

It was more than an excuse; it had been the first thing in her mind this morning.

"So you can't possibly have me," she said. "If I gave you the disease, you'd give it to your wife." She shuddered. "And if she's got a lover . . ."

133

He flinched from the final extension of her thought. Nevertheless, he put a strong hand to her shoulder, not attempting to embrace her, merely communicating the reassurance of a loving touch.

"It's not likely," he said quietly. "Those girls, they'd have to be pretty clean, I would think."

Her eyes were quick. "What do you know about it? Have *you* been there, too?"

"Of course not," he snapped. His tone relented. "I've heard other men talk about massage parlors."

"What happens in those places, anyhow? Just masturbation, or . . . or the whole thing?"

"Just about what you're willing to pay for, the way I understand it."

"What is it with men, that they need to have a place where they can buy sex?" she asked plaintively.

He gazed at the top of her head. *Because he's not getting it at home*, was the immediate thought in his male mind, engendered out of the revulsion for her that had crept unaware into his feelings. But of course he couldn't say it, even if the situation must be largely her fault.

"I don't know. Some men find it easier, I guess, more to their liking, to pay for it and forget about it."

She felt, then, the pressure of his hand, seeking to push her on her back. She resisted, thinking, That's all you want, too. Get your fuck, and get out of here.

"You *can't* want to make love," she said. "Not with the risk you'd be running of catching a disease."

He knew, as well as he had ever known anything, that if he didn't have her today he'd never get another chance. Or have the courage to take another chance, if it were offered.

The thought made him reckless of the consequences. "But I do. I do."

She gazed at her folded hands. "I . . . I feel *dirty*."

His voice came more strongly. "You've never felt like that with you and me. It's always been *right*."

"Not us. Him. His cock in me, after it's been in a whore's mouth, her cunt . . . I just feel dirty. All over."

He would have to lead her into forgiveness for her husband to restore her lust to be fucked by him.

"You've been with him after being with me," he pointed out. A risky thing, to make her aware of that simple fact. But it was the only point of attack he could think of against the shell she had built around herself.

"I had never gone to him from another man, not until you," she said defensively. "He must have been visiting the massage parlor for *years*."

"How do you know?"

"I know, that's all."

He did not understand, and she had to make him understand. Otherwise, it was all over between them. Something in her would not let it be over. Because *he* was all she had now.

Gazing straight into his face, she said, "What if your wife —what if you *knew* she had been with a lover, had come to you with the memory of a lover's cock warm in her flesh?"

It raised in him a small anger. "That's not very likely," he snapped.

"How do you *know?*" Her voice was cruelly subversive. "You don't know, you *can't* know your wife any better than I knew Hale." She gazed at him with stricken eyes. "No better than I know you, or you know me." She took a shattering breath. "That's the terrible thing about this world we live in. Everybody owns secret places in their souls they never let anybody into—mate, or friend, or lover."

His voice was stiff with rejection. "Eleanor has never looked at another man. I can assure you of that. Just because your husband . . ."

"I never had, either, until I met you," she said in that infuriating tone of certainty. "She might have met somebody yesterday, or ten years ago. She might meet somebody tomorrow."

She knew, with the love that remained in her heart, that out of her own hurt she was hurting him.

She didn't want to hurt him. She smiled wanly. "Here

I've come into this small room of our love bringing the whole big nasty world, haven't I?"

He made himself smile. "Yes. But I can hardly blame you."

"I made the rule. I was the first to break it," she said, self-accusatory. "I didn't have the right to do that."

"I gave you the right," he said warmly. "Because I love you."

She searched his face again. "Do you?"

His answer was as simple as her question. "Yes."

"Why?"

"I don't know. But I do."

Her voice still carried the burden of sadness. "Like I love you. Like I love Hale." She was silent for a moment. "Is it possible? I mean . . . to love two people at the same time?"

"I haven't quit loving my wife because I love you," he said strongly. "Just as you haven't quit loving your husband. If you *had* quit, it wouldn't matter what he's done."

She did not challenge him this time. She simply said it, in the simplest terms. "Then we must grant them the same possibility that exists in us. Something in Hale loves that whore."

She had not asserted again that Eleanor could, as easily as she, have a lover. Nevertheless, the unspoken words of the equation opened a door in his soul. Recalling the forthright manner in which Eleanor had come to him, those many years ago, he knew she would—could—choose a lover in the same way.

In this instant of time that was both a realization and an acceptance, he was ready to leave this woman unfucked and unloved. Because she was, he knew with whatever honesty remained in his soul, too demanding of honesty and truth. She wanted of him so much more than his cock, more than he could find in himself to give.

As though sensing his withdrawal, she put forth a familiar hand, pulled down the zipper, took out his cock to gaze upon it ruefully, yet with feminine appreciation. He stood bewitched, waiting for her next move.

136

Here is one man's cock I can taste, she told herself. Knowing it might have been in his wife's cunt last night, even this morning, doesn't make me *not* want to taste it. Why is it different with Hale?

She yearned, in this moment of truth, to put her mouth on him. So she did, her hands clasping his lean buttocks to pull him close. She took his cock greedily, felt it jerking in her mouth, growing mightily. She possessed the power over this great male organ.

If I ever have to earn my living, I could do it like this, she thought in a swift fantasy of having been summoned to this dingy motel room to perform upon him this service. The fantasy quickened her mouth, warmed her bought-and-paid-for cunt. He owned her for this hour, as Hale had owned the woman of the massage parlor.

She felt him beginning to thrust toward orgasm. Too quick, she was doing him too right. She deprived him of her mouth and looked up into his face, a secret smile showing faintly on her lips.

As she clasped his cock with a warm hand, stroking tantalizingly, she told him: "Put a hundred dollars on the bed, and I'll do exactly what you want me to do. *Everything* you want."

She held her breath, wondering if he would accept the reality of her fantasy. She read first in his eyes a baffled expression; then the sudden understanding. Her breath snatched convulsively in her throat as his hand reached for the wallet in his hip pocket.

His voice was hard, bargaining. "I won't give you more than fifty."

She was delighted with his prompt entry into the game.

"It has to be a hundred. That's my going price." She showed him an impish grin. Recklessly she added, "One hundred bills gives you the key to the front door and the key to the back door."

She was giving him her ass. Out of fantasy, true; but the act would be real. Somehow he could understand why she found it necessary today to sell her body to him, as a massage-parlor girl had sold *her* body to her husband. The

137

agility of her inventiveness, the intuitive genius of such a submission in her present state of feeling, literally took away his breath, made his cock throb eagerly in her teasing hand.

Fumbling in haste, he found the bills, dropped them fluttering to the bed. Releasing her grip, she grappled after the money. Then, clutching the bills in one hand, she fell backward on the bed, lifting her dress as she did so to reveal her naked flesh.

"Take that pussy, it's all yours," she said, the words a gasp of sheer lust.

Still clothed, he mounted her, driving hard into her depths. Fiery hot and dripping, her cunt was laid open to him, clutching at his cock like a tiny hand, yet yielding, yielding, depth after depth to his assault.

Immediately he felt the urge to come, he had to come, but he wouldn't let himself come. He wanted even more, out of stored-up anger, to punish her with his great cock until she cried out in anguish and ecstasy.

Like a chameleon of the flesh, she changed. She was suddenly *too* yielding, offering neither resistance nor response to his angry thrusts. The money clenched in her fist, her eyes searched his face as though she were a spectator. She was, he sensed, exploring a sensation she had not experienced before.

It was wonderful. It was awful. For the first time since Billy-Bob, she had surrendered control. She had *sold* her body for the money clutched in her hand, making him free to do with her as he willed, in all anger as in all lust. She could feel in the drive of his fierce tool the primitive, unthinking male aggressiveness that for eons of time civilization has papered over—without ever quite destroying it—with chivalry and romance and social politeness. It was *this* that she had once encountered with the animal named Billy-Bob. Now she, of her own will, had made herself helpless again before it.

This is why Hale goes to that massage-parlor girl, she told herself. He can own her as he has never owned me. He has always known in his soul that only one man has ever owned me; his best friend, Billy-Bob Radley. He has never been able to forgive me for Billy-Bob; and *this* he could never forgive me, either, because I have sold myself, I am *owned*, and I love it, I hate it; it is primitive and real, hurting me in my soul while I love it in my body.

"Come, damn you, come!" *he* snarled through gritted teeth. His groin slammed against her mount more fiercely yet, the great shaft ramrodding into depths she had never given to Hale, had never given *him* until now. Experiencing the ultimate surrender, she fled helplessly through one writhing orgasm after the other.

He was grinning triumphantly now. In a stroke of terror, she knew why; suddenly his cock withdrew, and immediately his strong hands forced her over on her belly.

One hand was pressing under her fork to lift her buttocks into position for the new assault. *NO!* she screamed silently, thinking she was screaming out loud. *PLEASE!* But he had bought her ass and his cock was pushing ruthlessly against the back door. She couldn't help it, she tightened like a clenched fist; then the great cock split her, like a cold knife, and she was still screaming silently.

Thinking the sound was in her mouth, as in her head, she remembered dimly that they were in a motel room, with people all around. If she kept on screaming, their rendezvous would be shamefully discovered. But it was hurting, oh God, how it hurt! Reaching a frantic hand for a pillow, she buried her mouth in it, smothering the scream into a pitiful whimper that surely *he* would heed.

But his cock, terrible in the ravaging strength of its need, had broken through, it was rammed tightly into her clenched rectum. She felt her bowels shuddering, she was terrified that she would make an awful mess, it had to quit hurting, it *had* to. But it didn't quit, it only got worse, when she had believed it couldn't possibly hurt any more than it was hurting already.

Wonderful, he told himself. *Wonderful*. Though his cock ached from battering against the barrier, the resistance of her tightening sphincter only drove him to a greater frenzy. He would have to hit her with his fist if she didn't give it to him! He had not ever struck a woman; something in him cringed at the thought even as some ruthless force doubled his fist in readiness.

Then: Her ass had yielded its sacred precincts, he was driving deep, it was *his*, he was taking what no man had ever taken, goddamn women anyway with their "Noes" and their "Maybes."

This is how a man ought to use a woman, he thought triumphantly. Break her down all the way. He couldn't blame that poor son-of-a-bitch of a husband for going to a whore. *She* had never let him be a total man. Hale had fucked her for twenty years, but he had never got a cherry.

He could feel the cold sweat oozing on her skin, hear her grunting moans as his cock grew mightier in preparation for the orgasm of his life. Until, without warning, he came so violently it shook his whole frame.

The ejaculation, a small volcano, exploded in her rectum. Letting go the final resistance, her ass warmed and bloomed as she flattened under him in a final surrender. She was bathed in a clammy sweat; yet, now that she had yielded the last fortress, there was in her a curious peacefulness.

How the damned male had loved it—the thought was a wryly secret triumph of her own—he was finished now, as no woman had ever finished him, but he wouldn't get out; his cock, miraculously still hard, was moving smoothly in long, easy strokes, celebrating his damned male victory. He did not know, in his triumph, that she had discovered in total surrender a secret female triumph of her own.

He fucked her gently, the sweetness in his soul as strong as honey on the tongue. Her ass began moving, backing up into his groin against each lazy stroke. A lovely sensation, to feel the silky softness of her buttocks snugged against the curve of his belly; it made him want to come again, sooner than he had expected.

Since he could do exactly as he pleased, he decided that this time it would please him to come in her cunt. His hands twirled her under him and, scarcely missing a beat, he was fucking her again, long and slow and easy, fucking true and forever.

He could see on her face the trace marks of tears, how she had bitten her lip raw. Her eyes avoided his, she turned aside her shattered face. Because he had used her as no man had used her before, he felt a deeply moved tenderness. Sensing that all capacity for orgasm had been whipped out of her exhausted flesh, generously, into her sweet, warm lassitude, he came in a solitary finishing ejaculation, feeling it flow as though a tap had been opened.

He rose up from her. He saw her eyes follow his cock, her features twisting in a grimace of disgust. Looking down, he saw blood mixed with brown smears, ringlike around the base of his shaft. On trembling legs he hurried into the bathroom. As he washed thoroughly, he felt a momentary disgust, with himself as with her. But it had, by God, been great . . . the greatest. He was not about to deny how fulfilling it had been.

When he returned, she was sitting up, staring at the bills crumpled in her hand.

"All right?" he asked with love.

"I hated it," she said. "It hurt worse than having a baby."

"There at the end, when you finally relaxed, it was much better, wasn't it?"

"No," she said shortly.

She stood up, pulled the rumpled dress over her head, dropped it to the floor, and walked into the bathroom. She was in the shower for a long time.

When she came out, toweling off, she could show him a wan smile. "Well, lover. You got the last cherry I'll ever have."

Her attempt at humor moved him profoundly. Holding out his arms, he said, "Come here, you lovely bitch."

She came to him, naked and used as she was, and his arms enfolded her, holding her with such a great cherishing that she began to weep.

It was, she realized, what she had longed to do since the devastating moment when she had glimpsed Hale going up

141

those secret stairs to a betrayal of her womanhood. Weeping had not been in her until this man, who had abused her flesh but now cherished it with love, had released also her final surrender to the grief and loss she had experienced during this terrible week.

She clung to him, the weeping like a long, slow overdue rain on the parched earth of her soul. Murmuring meaningless and comforting words, he stroked her naked flesh with an understanding love, he held her, he cherished her, until the tears were finished, leaving her empty and exhausted and at peace.

"Better now?" he whispered.

The silent answer was the creeping-closer of her body, so small and vulnerable. He held her, knowing that this woman was the great woman of his life; she possessed depths and territories it would take forever to explore. And so he told her, and told her again; until finally, with a fucking as sweetly gentle as if it were the first time love between Man and Woman had existed on this earth, she believed him, and was content.

Yet, at the parting—though he expected it as a matter of course now that they had worked through the fantasy-game into an entirely new order of themselves—she did not offer to return the hundred dollars. Instead, a secret smile on her face, she smoothed the crumpled bills and tucked them neatly into her purse.

The Man:

Beyond the sheer wonder at the satisfying complexity of woman he had today experienced, one strong emotion remained with him. It was the last feeling, now or ever, he would have expected to encounter within his soul.

Her words had planted a seed of suspicion so deeply it could not be dislodged. Foremost in his mind as he entered his home was an evil speculation: Had Eleanor really been playing duplicate bridge all afternoon? On *any* of the Thursday afternoons?

He stood in the kitchen, the emptiness of the house thick about him. Immediately he pushed away the unworthy thought.

Only to discover a deeper thought hidden beneath it. *He knew nothing of the separate life Eleanor had lived all these years they had been married.*

There is, he reminded himself protectively, the life we share, truly one life; it always has been, always will be. She wants me to become president of the bank as strongly as I do. She has been conscientious in providing the solid foundation for that achievement: A good home, a reasonably happy marriage, a perfect family life, a strong relationship with her father, a social structure centered around the bank family. As I have applied myself to the duties and responsibilities of each position I have held on the ladder reaching upward to that crowning eminence.

There were, he recognized now, definite boundaries around each carefully shaped phase of their joint existence. One—the necessary solitude which he devoted to preserving the youthful vigor of his good body—had been openly marked out by himself. Another, unknown to Eleanor, had kept secret his daydreams of perfect sex. But—other walls had been erected by Eleanor to protect her inviolate turf of bridge club and out-of-town tournaments, that whole social milieu in which she would eventually become a life master.

As he had not, this afternoon, devoted himself to the advertised bicycle jaunt, so Eleanor might as well not have shuffled the first deck of cards.

He went to the bar, mixed a strong drink. It was the height of irony, he realized, to dwell on such suspicions immediately after he had passed the afternoon in a grand and glorious fucking. Completely illogical, yet undeniable. Especially now that he had become an unfaithful husband, he needed to trust in Eleanor's fidelity as the cement holding together the world whose destruction he risked every time he fucked that woman.

In an effort toward self-protection from these dangerous thoughts, his mind veered to *her*. What a marvelous fuck she had made of herself today! Taking the hundred dollars, she had become totally submissive to his most secret desire . . . when, the time before, she had held him down with the strength of her need to dominate until he had reacted in panic.

Each facet of their fucking, he recognized, was a part of him, as it was a part of her. The taking of her back-door cherry had been the most sexually fulfilling act of his life since the night Eleanor had come to his apartment, told him she meant to marry him, and sucked him off.

During these years, doing him with her mouth had remained Eleanor's greatest sexual artistry. Involuntarily he wondered—if she *did* go to bed with other men —whether she put her mouth on them also with such deep lust.

At this wounding juncture in his thinking, Eleanor returned, greeting him with her usual quiet welcome as she passed on beyond into the bedroom. He stood gripping his glass, gazing after her, mind aflame with suspicion.

Did she move like a well-fucked woman? Returning from a bridge joust, she carried always such an air of self-satisfaction. Win or lose, it seemed to satisfy a need in her nothing else could. What if it isn't contract bridge that fulfills her? he thought darkly, but the residual warmth of another man's cock in her satisfied cunt?

He gulped down the drink, fixed another. Suppose I

144

should confront her with my suspicions? he thought suddenly. As quickly—for he knew Eleanor—he knew the answer: She would answer to any accusation with the simple truth, yea or nay.

He wavered, not sure if he could bear the truth. He knew fatefully that, if her answer should confirm his suspicions, it would shatter his life beyond redemption.

He recognized, now, something about himself he had not realized before—because, quite simply, he had never looked at it. Indeed, his existence for years had been patterned on *not* looking, *not* knowing, *not* being aware.

Since the day she had come into his life, Eleanor had dominated him. Eleanor had directed his every acquiescent move as surely as *she* had pinned him on his back in the station wagon and fucked him out of her own will.

As with *her*, something in him had accepted—had *loved*, had *needed*—to be so dominated by Eleanor.

The realization rudely jarred his sensibility as a man. His attraction to *her* had been, he saw now, the first small step toward that realization. Now he knew; knowing, he would never forget.

So what now, little man? he thought.

He stood frozen, hating *her* for opening him to such a terrible realization. I even took it out in taking care of the body, he told himself demeaningly. I made myself proud of the flesh because I knew my soul had sold out.

He thought of the sweating dedication to physical strength, the sweet ache of tired muscles . . . while, all the time, his inner spirit, his *manhood*, had become flabby, sapped of strength, through neglect and disuse.

The telephone rang, startling him. Instead of waiting for Eleanor to answer, as he usually did, he snatched up the kitchen extension.

Eleanor had picked up, also. "Oh, hello, Norma," she said cheerily. "How did you and your partner do today? I didn't get a chance to ask before I left."

He listened to Norma's explanation of disaster as patiently as did Eleanor. At the end, Eleanor clucked in commiseration, adding, "Well, I didn't *expect* anything when Paul couldn't make it. You know, I play better with Paul than anybody. There's some sort of ESP communication between us . . ."

He was ashamed to stand here in the kitchen eavesdropping on the innocuous chitchat. Until *she* had aroused his suspicions—simply because, for God's sake, her husband had taken his male needs to a massage parlor—it would never have occurred to him. For years, Eleanor had conducted a lively telephone social life.

"But I did decide one thing," Eleanor was saying, tiny in his ear. "I *am* going to that tournament next week. Even if it is three days."

"Can your husband go with you for that long?" Norma asked doubtfully. "Overnight is one thing, but . . ."

"Oh, he never goes; he'd be bored out of his head," Eleanor said quickly. "I've made up my mind about something else, too. If we win, I'm planning to go on to the big tournament in San Francisco." She chuckled again. "I've *never* done that. So I'm putting myself into training. This time, I mean to go all the way!"

"How wonderful for you, Eleanor!" Norma gushed.

He hung up, thoroughly disgusted with himself. He put down his half-finished drink, walked into the living room. He could hear Eleanor's voice chatting on, maintaining her social life. *Being Eleanor.*

It's only my own guilt at being unfaithful, he assured himself. I let *her* spill her personal bitterness over her broken marriage into *my* marriage. I'll never again listen to her, not for a second. Just fuck her good and come away home, like a man ought to do.

He had continued to listen with one ear to Eleanor; she was now dialing a call. He could not stop himself; he was again in the kitchen, waiting tensely for the connection before, with great care, he eased the kitchen extension off the hook.

". . . let me down, Paul," he heard Eleanor saying. "You could have let me know, at least."

"Sorry, love, something important came up at the last

146

minute," the man's voice said languidly. "How did you play?"

"You know I never play as well if you're not my partner," Eleanor said reproachfully.

His breath gusted with relief from the tension the sound of a male voice had created. Paul had, after all, addressed Eleanor as "love." Merely a bridge partner; probably gay, at that, to be playing afternoon bridge with a bunch of women.

"Well, anyway, I've made up my mind," Eleanor said briskly. "I am definitely committing us to the three-day tournament." Her voice changed subtly. "That is, if *you* can make it."

"Three days, that's risky, isn't it? You've never . . ."

Her voice became urgent. "*Three days*, Paul. Three days to play bridge, three nights to . . . to be together."

The enticement of tone, the blatant meaning, froze his soul. Numbly he registered the cajoling shift into a lustful coarseness as she said, in a huskier voice, "I'll wear your beautiful cock down to the nub, Paul. I'll put you to sleep every night doing what you love best. Say you'll go, dear. You know you can if you wish, you don't have to go to a job every day like other men."

"But we've always been so careful," Paul protested. "What if *he* . . ."

"*He* never has had the least suspicion. So why should he start now?" she asked cruelly. "Don't worry about *that*." She laughed, a lubricious sound. "And you don't have a wife anymore to worry about. So there's no earthly reason . . ."

"All right, all right," Paul said, chuckling. "Three days is obviously what you intend to have. So I surrender, my dear."

Trembling, he leaned against the kitchen wall. The telephone still at his ear, he listened to Eleanor crooning at the man Paul, her lover, telling him in lewd detail what she meant to do to him for three whole days together.

Only one Paul in their social circle fit her description of a man who had no need to go to business every day. The only son of the richest family in town, a player of tennis and golf, a sailor in regattas on the nearby reservoir. Young —no more than thirty-five—languid and blasé, married three times, with a terrible reputation built on the conquest of other men's wives.

His soul was stunned. Despite the arousal of his suspicions, something deeply secure in him had not believed his wife could possibly be unfaithful. Had been *smug* in not believing it.

When—it had been so simple to find out. The thought of how easy discovery had been stabbed him into action. Dropping the telephone, on stiff legs he stalked through the living room. He slammed open the bedroom door, stood glaring at his wife.

Eleanor, after one startled glance, said something breathless into the receiver and hung up.

"You . . ." he said. "You . . ." His voice strangled, died in his throat.

She rose, her tone accusatory as though his fault overshadowed her own. "You've been listening to my telephone calls."

On the stiff legs, he advanced. "You . . . it was Paul Robards you were talking to."

Retreating, she turned her back, going to her side of the bed to pick up a pack of cigarettes. He watched her extract one and light it, thinking irrelevantly that she knew he didn't like cigarette smoke in the house, especially in the bedroom, so she smoked much less than she used to.

She turned to blow smoke into the air between them. Her tone was light, amused. "My darling, I've had a dozen lovers over the years. Paul is only the latest."

Her careless tone chilled him colder than ever. "But . . . why, Eleanor?"

She blew smoke again. "Darling, you've had your little chippies all along. So why do you wish to deny me *my* private pleasures?"

"No!" he shouted. "My God, no! If you think . . ."

She showed him a mocking smile. "Then what's all that keep-forever-young bit, darling? I never knew a middle-aged man to work so hard at keeping a body the young things will deign to lust after."

He was strangling again with baffled fury. Anger, at least, was a cleansing thing, wiping out his guilt over eavesdropping as well as the deeper guilt about *her*.

He wanted to hurt Eleanor. Physically. In an instantaneous imagining, he saw his fist crash into her face, wiping away that superior smile. Through sheer male brutality, he could regain control of the situation.

It would be, he knew as quickly, only a temporary solution to a long-standing situation. A *dozen lovers*. Over how many years of ostensibly happy marriage? Which meant that what he had believed to be the truth of their lives was instead a living lie. Not only for the world; for him.

Eleanor, tensed against the fury so plain in his face, had been watching him warily. Sensing that the moment of crisis had passed, she turned away to snuff out the cigarette.

"But . . . *Paul Robards*," he said helplessly. "You knew his reputation."

"Yes, Paul was quite a challenge . . . as you were once a challenge," she said casually. "But, aside from all else, he's a *marvelous* bridge player, the partner I've needed for years to win some really major tournaments and get my life master rating at last."

His heart fell. "Then . . . you're going to leave me . . ."

She chuckled at his simple-mindedness. "Of course not, darling. I wouldn't *think* of marrying Paul. Do you think I want to be sitting at home, like all his wives have had to do, while Paul is out screwing other women? Paul is not, never has been and never will be, marriage material."

"But when I'm gone . . ."

"You're not going anywhere, darling."

The bland assumption fired his anger again. "You don't think I'll put up with this, do you?"

"Of course you will, darling." Still that confident tone of

149

utter control. "Because you want to be president of the bank as much as I want you to be president."

The statement stopped him cold. Knowing him better than he knew himself, she had spoken the simple truth. Much of his dismay, the sense of betrayal, was attributable to the loss of his career, not the irredeemable loss of his wife.

So where does that leave love, the habit of a lifetime together? he thought in disillusionment. The tenderness, the common goals we have shared? Lies. All lies.

Eleanor chose me, that long time ago, as much for a future president of her father's bank as for husband and father. She probably even talked it over with dear old "Daddy" before showing up for the first time alone at my apartment.

He experienced, in that shattered moment, an almost irresistible urge to tell her about the woman he had been with this afternoon. *That* would wipe the superior smile from her face! Not the "little chippies" she had believed him capable of screwing throughout their years together; a great love, the love of a lifetime, a woman to go to when he walked out on her.

As, he told himself, *I will walk out*.

The words of proud confession were shaped and ready in his mind. Let Eleanor know there can be real love, not just random and temporary lust. Crush her by the knowledge of how far he had gone from her.

He did not speak the fatal message. For, looking at his wife, standing firm in all strength and certitude, a tiny voice whispered cruelly in his mind: *What if, when you tell her, she doesn't care?*

Indeed, she was studying him now with a certain curiosity. "Were you really telling the truth, darling, when you swore that you haven't had your lovers, too?"

Numbly, he nodded. The only words available to him were the words of the confession he could not make.

She shook her head. "I'd have sworn, the way you worked at keeping the old bod in shape, you were after young stuff. I didn't mind all that much, really—as long as you were discreet enough not to endanger your career, or our position in this town."

"Eleanor," he said hoarsely. "You are a monster."

At last he had stirred her; anger edged her voice. "I am the woman you married," she said harshly. "I knew then that you were marrying Daddy's bank as much as you were me. I didn't care. I wanted to have you—*own* you—and if it took the bank to do it, I could accept that."

She put out a hand toward him, gripped it into a fist. "I *do* own you, my darling. I always have, I always will. Because you *like* being owned by Eleanor. Go screw a few horny girls, I don't care as long as you keep your nose clean. I know you'll always come back; you'll *have* to, because I'm the only woman who can give you what you want more than anything else."

"You really believe it, don't you?" he said, helplessly, recognizing the truth but unable to accept it.

His voice had choked on him. He started again. "You think I'll go on like I've always done, knowing that you and Paul Robards are lovers, living with it, accepting it." He stared at her guiltless face. "You haven't even changed your mind about going off with him next week, have you?"

"Of course not, darling," she said. "Did you think I would, just because you know about it?"

"I'm leaving," he said hoarsely. "Believe it or not, *I am leaving*. Right now."

"You'll come back," she said confidently. "Once you've considered the alternatives." Her eyes were hard, direct. "You will realize that you're not just leaving evil old Eleanor, my dear. You'll be leaving Daddy, too. Leaving the bank."

He stood wavering, baffled, wanting only to get away from her once and for all. He had always recognized the strength of her will. The strength of her sexual desires. He had never realized, however, that her mind possessed the same ruthless streak that had sustained her father through a long lifetime of business success.

Incredibly, her tone shifted toward cajolery as she moved toward him, saying, "You're terribly more attractive now, my darling, than you've been in years. Isn't that strange? Now that you *know* me, I want you to take me, *knowing* . . ."

She came closer, too close, her hand strongly gripping his crotch. "I'll show you all over again how good I can be," she whispered intensely. "Just relax, my darling, relax, and let me . . ."

She was sinking to her knees, his cock between her hands; then her mouth came upon him. He could not believe it, but it was rising with the memory and the promise of her marvelous mouth. Though he knew he was surrendering supinely to deliberate enticement, for one instant he yielded to the pulsation of her sucking mouth, knowing that, next, she would fuck him.

If he yielded so far, it would restore between them everything that had been lost. Except . . . except for the terrible knowledge forever in his soul that, because he was in thrall to his own ambitions and desires, he was her slave.

A terrible pain from her raking teeth as he tore himself away; he fled from the pain as he fled from her, blundering into the living room and across the kitchen, to slam through the door into the garage. Fumbling for his keys as he slid behind the wheel of his car, he hit the button and backed in a tight curve that swept the hood around to face the street. Shifting into forward gear, he floored the accelerator and roared into the street, the light car careening on the turn.

He was free now, free of Eleanor, free of all that his life had been. There was left to him only *her*, the only possible rescue from the debacle of his world.

He didn't care who answered the phone. He had to talk to *her*. Now.

He let it ring, ring again and again until he heard the receiver being lifted. He braced himself against the challenge of a man's voice, trying frantically to think how to get past the husband to his great love.

He heaved a sigh of relief. *Her* voice, saying, "Yes?" He could read her tone as a woman, securely at home, who expected only an inconsequential telephone call from a friend.

"It's me," he said, choking out the words.

She gasped and instinctively lowered the level of her voice. "What are you doing, calling here?"

"Can you talk?" he asked urgently.

"Yes, Hale isn't home yet, though I expect him any minute . . ."

He gripped the telephone. "I've got to see you. Now."

Her voice was cool, firm. "You know I can't do that."

She had to understand. Once she understood, her great love would answer greatly to his need.

"You were right about Eleanor," he said, holding his voice calm with a great effort. "She's had a dozen lovers. It was the easiest thing in the world to find out she's been betraying me all these years, so easy; she didn't make the least effort to keep her telephone conversations secret."

A great bitterness in that; so confident of his gullibility, she had been contemptuously careless. So *secure,* so *strong.*

Her voice was a breath of sound. "Oh, I'm so sorry . . ."

"That's why I've got to see you. Now. Tonight."

Alarm. "I can't possibly get out."

"Listen," he said desperately. "Will you . . . will you pack a bag, go away with me?"

Silence. He had hit her with it too suddenly. But —though the idea had not, until this moment, dwelled even briefly in his mind—it was the right thing. For him. For the two of them. He felt a breath of liberation sweeping through his soul. To hell with Eleanor. To hell with the bank. To hell with everything but *her.* And himself.

Her voice revealed an equal desperation. "I can't, my love. I *can't.*"

"You mean you won't," he said bluntly.

"I hear Hale's car," she said hastily. "I've got to hang up."

"Do you love me?" he said, playing the last card, thinking that he knew the only possible answer. But he had been so wrong, so many times . . . He held his breath, waiting.

"Yes," she said. "Yes. Listen, he's in the carport now, he's coming in . . ."

"I'm going to the cabin," he said in a last desperate grasp at hope. "You know how to get there. I'll be waiting."

"Don't," she said agonizingly. "I can't come tonight. You know I can't."

His voice was firm. "I'll wait until you do come. However long it takes."

He heard a man's voice in cheerful greeting, then she hung up, cutting him off. Cutting him off . . . forever?

The Two:

He had given up on the waiting. Sitting on the tiny dock, he stared bleakly out over the small lake, telling himself for the hundredth time there was nothing left to do but go back to Eleanor, back to the bank, and do the best he could with what was left of his life.

He had actually risen to climb the hill when he heard the sound of a motor. Probably Eleanor, he told himself heavily, she doesn't give up easily. Eleanor would know that the cabin was the only place he would have to go.

When he had climbed high enough to see the familiar station wagon, his heart leaped. Belated though she was, *she* had come to him. Bringing a whole new life.

Her heart aching for him, she watched him climbing toward where she waited. But when, without a word, he put his arms around her, she felt herself stiff and unyielding within the embrace. She had kept telling herself that she would not—*could* not—respond to his wild plea . . . right up until the time, after noon, when she had got into the station wagon to drive to the cabin.

Such a *shattered* look to him; it made her realize, for the first time, how fragile men are, so much more fragile than women in these matters of love and fidelity.

She drew away, hoping she could establish a necessary distance in a manner that would not signal itself as a rejection.

"I came only to talk."

He looked at her; he saw in her a vast difference from the woman she had become in his arms. The remoteness, which he had destroyed so effectively, had become once more her shield.

"I don't want to talk. I want to fuck," he said, knowing that he must first penetrate her, spiritually as well as physically. Make her his again, as only yesterday she had been his.

She turned away abruptly, to gaze out over the glimpse of lake below. "I can't do that, either."

She had become aware this morning of the belated flow of her blood. A week late, despite the IUD, and she had worried that his strong and abundant semen might have overridden the barrier. She had checked the beads, found them in place, but that was little reassurance—she had heard of women becoming pregnant despite the IUD.

Then, immediately, she had thought in sadness: My last period was the first Thursday we planned to meet. This great love, then, had been encompassed within one menstrual cycle, one movement of the moon, the burgeoning and shedding of a single egg within her ovaries.

The time-of-love had dwelled in her soul as an eternity. But now, she knew in sadness, they had reached the other side of forever. And so, for the first time, she admitted to her understanding the truth that their beautiful love, their raging lust, had an end as predestined as the beginning.

It was—in her soul, her heart, her female flesh—a terrible sensing of the mortality that dwells at the core of all human love. As there is a time for waxing and fruition into a self-contained whole, so there is also the time for waning, and a final end.

For this brief span, they had dwelled privately in their erotic Garden of Eden, in which all was perfect love and perfect lust. Inevitably, however, the Serpent of Knowledge had entered: The irrevocable discovery that other people—*her* husband, *his* wife . . . indeed, all human beings—carry within them also a web of fantasy-dreams as essential to them as her fantasy-dreams had been to her.

Only then had she known that she must go to *him*, in an effort to make him understand, as she now understood, that an ending had been inevitable in their beginning. Because, she told herself, our love required perfection, in a perfect isolation from reality. Perfection—when, if we had not been terribly flawed human beings, we could not have come together in the first instance.

Now, standing before him, explaining, "It's that time of month," she felt also a saving tenderness for this man of her brief passage from one menstrual cycle to the next. This tenderness would be the only enduring profit for her soul.

She could read in him the immediate disappointment. Yet she sensed, somehow, that the act of lust was not as important to him at this moment as he claimed it to be. No, she thought. He needs more . . . more, I think, than I can give. But I can only try.

She went to him, put both arms around his waist. "Let's go inside. We can be together anyway, drink coffee, talk . . ." She made a small laugh. "At least I've brought your sheets back."

She opened the car door, took out the neatly folded sheets, and carrying them over her arm, led the way into the cabin as though she were the hostess. In the kitchen, she began looking through cabinets for the coffee and the coffeepot.

He sat at the table, watching in a blankness of understanding. He *knew* that body moving so lithely about the room. Only yesterday he had *owned* that body, as he had owned her soul. Today, she had become again a stranger.

He was silent while she made coffee, poured it, placed a cup before him and sat down opposite, saying in simplicity, "Now tell me."

He told her, in excruciating detail. She listened without watching his face because unshed tears showed in his eyes.

"The worst thing, it was so *easy* to find her out," he ended the telling in an awkward agony. "She didn't make the least effort to be clever. She called Paul Robards from our bedroom while I was in the kitchen. Any time, over the years we've been married, I could have found out through a simple awareness of what was going on under my nose."

She raised her head. "Maybe it's better *not* to pry. It's so terrible to know the truth about someone you love."

"I don't love Eleanor anymore," he said violently.

She shook her head. Firmly. "But you do." Her hand crept out to touch his hand, flaccid on the table. "You don't want to leave your wife. Any more than I want to leave my husband."

His violent movement shoved the chair backward, to

crash unheeded against the floor. "But I *have* left her." He leaned toward her, both hands braced flat on the tabletop. "We're leaving *everything* in this town behind, you and I. We'll be together all the time, we'll . . ." His breath stumbled against the words. He forced them into speech. "As soon as we can get our divorces, we'll be married."

He retrieved the chair. He did not sit down, but stood listening to her low, steady reply.

"And how long will it be before we begin to find hatred inside our loving lust for each other's bodies? Because we'll have both given up too much."

He started to speak. She held up a hand to forestall him. "You must know, my love, that all during that week before we fucked for the first time, half the time I was convinced that, for you, I was just another conquest. Another 'quick piece of ass.'" Her hand held him silent. "Just like you, I'm sure, kept telling yourself that my getting laid by another man wouldn't be anything new. To be so ready and waiting for you, I must have done it a dozen times."

He sank into his seat. Those words, "another quick piece of ass," had struck at his conscience. Her voice went on inexorably, merciless and loving.

"How long will it be before we begin to doubt each other's fidelity? You know how capable *I* am of unfaithfulness. I know only too well that one chance meeting with a woman can lead you into adultery. We wouldn't have even the support of old habit, old love, that we knew with Hale and with Eleanor."

The words were cruel. The words were loving. They penetrated his soul, flowering there in a harsh and painful light where only the darkling turmoil of agony had dwelled.

He said quietly, "You're telling me that we, neither one of us, have the right to blame them. We loved each other, we needed each other. Because of that love and that need, we've yielded all right to hold them accountable for *their* actions."

She nodded.

"But—Eleanor has had a dozen lovers. She told me so. Over I don't know how many years of our marriage.

Because, she claimed, she was quite sure I was enjoying 'little chippies' on the side. But I wasn't. I wasn't. So she started it. I didn't."

"I don't know how long Hale has been going to a massage parlor, either. The *number* of times he's needed to pay for it doesn't make any difference."

He watched her. "You haven't confronted him with it?"

She shook her head. "No."

"You're not going to?"

She drew a deep breath. "No. I don't think so."

He looked at her hands, so still on the table. "Women, somehow, can handle unfaithfulness better than a man can. Something in a woman will accept that a man's cock has been in a strange cunt. But when a man thinks about another man's cock rampaging in his wife's pussy . . ."

Her eyes were bleak on his face. "Don't think it didn't ruin my soul. Just as it ruined yours."

He looked away, saying, "I don't see how I can keep on living with Eleanor. Even the idea of her mouth on me again . . ."

Something inside her relaxed; he had accepted, without knowing it yet, that they would not go away together.

She put her hand on his hand, clutching it hard. "That's how I felt," she said sympathetically. "At first. But old habit, old love, is hard to break. You find yourself going on, you even forget that you *are* going on beyond the terrible thing that happened."

He was watching her. "You love me so *much*, don't you? But I'd have to kidnap you to make you leave town with me."

She nodded, and sighed. "We should have known, at the beginning, that it would be only a sometime thing." She smiled sadly. "A beautiful thing, but fragile as a butterfly, dancing for an hour among the flowers, not knowing it was born out of dirt, and doomed to enter again into dirt when its little dance is done."

"I don't know what I'll do without you," he said tragically. "I can't even remember the kind of man I was before I met you."

"Nor I the kind of woman," she agreed, her hand tightening. "You've been so good—and so bad—for me. As I suppose I have been good and bad for you."

"Would you have missed it?" he asked, because he had to ask.

She gazed thoughtfully into his eyes. "I don't know," she said slowly.

Feeling her now, remembering her vividly in the throes of lust, a stirring warmth crept through his groin.

"We're sitting here talking about not seeing each other anymore. Aren't we?"

Sudden tears sparkled in her eyes. "Yes. That's what we're talking about."

He got up. He came around the table, lifted her chin with a cupped palm, kissed her deeply on the mouth.

"Then we've got to fuck one more time."

She moved away from the temptation of his lips. "But I told you. I can't. It's the wrong time of month."

"To hell with 'the wrong time of month.'"

He registered her physical revulsion at the thought of being fucked in her blood. With a sinking of his heart, he knew it could not, today, be the good thing it would have to be to stand as their last time in each other's flesh.

"Then we must meet again," he said. "Next Thursday."

She stirred uneasily. "Let's not string it out, darling. Let's not try to keep it going past the point where it ought to stop. It's the worst thing we could do to ourselves."

His voice was forceful. "We can't let the last time be the *last* time. That one was all for me. The *last time* has got to be for both of us."

Her very flesh was trembling toward surrender. In an act of the will, she closed herself against the temptation.

"You must make your peace with your wife, as I've made my peace with Hale. After that, you won't *want* to have me again."

"Yes," he said. "I will always lust for you."

"All right, I know it, I will always lust for you, too."

"Then will you come—Next Thursday—as always?"

"Always?" she said wryly. "It's only been a month."

Then, in an abrupt turn he could not follow except as an evasion, she asked: "Have you told your wife about us?"

"No."

"Are you going to?"

"No."

She breathed more deeply. "I was sure you had told her. A revenge, at least, for what she's been doing to you all these years."

"I wanted to," he said painfully. "I meant to. But—I don't believe she'd even care."

Her smile was more like a grimace. "Just as I couldn't tell Hale about us—no more than I could accuse him of the massage parlor."

"Like you said. We haven't left ourselves much ground to stand on."

She could even smile. "Guilty minds in guilty bodies."

He went to the stove. "More coffee?"

"Yes. Please."

He brought the pot, poured for both of them, and sat down across the table. They were comfortable together in the sudden domesticity, tinged though it was by the sadness of departure.

"We have, at least, given each other the best of ourselves," she said reminiscently. "You shared somehow in my fantasies, in a way Hale never did. As I shared in yours."

"Yes," he said.

"I never once gave Hale the best of me," she said thoughtfully. "For the silliest of reasons—because I've always lusted for a hairy man. Isn't that silly?"

"Not if it was real," he said.

She said quickly, "It was real. Because of Billy-Bob, you know, the boy who fucked me for the first time. *Raped* me. Billy-Bob was hairier than you are."

She stopped talking. Then she said, "I invited it, you know. Something inside me knew even at eighteen that, if I were going to spend my life with Hale, I had to have a hairy man first. I invited it. And I loved it. When it was rape."

"Have you ever had rape fantasies?" he asked, remembering how she had reacted when he had taken her from behind.

She shook her head. "Never had to. I *lived* that one." She sighed again. "Humans are such strange animals." She looked at him. "How long before you'll have another woman?"

He was startled. "What do you mean? After you, there can't *be* another woman."

Her smile was wise, sad with the wisdom. "We're both capable of it. We know that now. It can happen again. To me. To you. So, probably, it *will* happen. Because the human heart can't stop searching for someone to love, someone to lust after."

He bowed his head. "Yes. I see. It *could* happen again."

This afterglow of love and lust had segued somehow into a species of happiness as they shared these last moments of time together. So she rose, saying, "I must go now." She paused to gaze at him. "I can tell you now," she said quietly. "I *wouldn't* have missed it. Not for anything. Even with the pain . . ."

She stopped talking because there was nothing left to say. He wanted to ask her again to see him one last time. But in him, as in her, nothing remained to be said.

He rose. He put his arms around her. He held her, as she held him. "Go well, my love," he whispered, and her voice echoed, "Go well. I hope at least I'll be a good memory. I know you'll be a good memory for me."

They walked, arms around waists, to the cars. He felt curiously peaceful, yet with a great regret. She shared his sunset feeling so easily that they did not have to speak it aloud, as they had explored verbally so many things in their time together. Ideas and feelings, she knew, he had never been able to talk about with anyone until her; as she had not been able to talk about them with anyone until him.

"I'll follow you down to the highway," he said.

They embraced, they kissed deeply, they drew apart. She got behind the wheel of the station wagon, ran it forward the distance allowable, twisted the wheel three times before she could get turned around.

On the cliff's edge of departure, she studied him through the windshield. He was wearing the same clothes he had worn yesterday, wrinkled now, crumpled and dirty. Right now he wants, more than anything, a hot shower and fresh clothes, she thought. And love. And lust. And understanding of himself as a man.

She put her head out the side window. "Next Thursday, then?" she called. She was rewarded by a wonderful smile of reprieve. "Next Thursday, for both of us," she said again, her voice surer than before.

She gave him a wicked grin. "I mean to taste that sweet cock just one more time."

The Man:

He had been waiting a long time when Eleanor came home, drinking steadily while he waited, without the least perceptible effect.

Eleanor stopped short when she saw him sitting in the living room. Then she came forward, dropping her purse into a chair.

"Daddy called this morning, wondering why you weren't at your desk," she told him in a neutral voice.

He regarded her, wondering if she had come from Paul. He couldn't tell if she had fucked today. A random thought meandered through his head: There ought to be a signal, a little red light, maybe, on top of people's heads that turns on when you fuck and doesn't go out for, say, twenty-four hours. It would make for a world so much more honest than the world we've got. That's for sure.

"What did you tell him?"

"Oh, I knew you'd be back, so I made up an excuse." She gave him an accusing stare. "I must say, I've never had to make your excuses to Daddy before. I warn you: I won't do it again."

He ignored her. "So you knew I'd be back."

She sat down on the far end of the sofa. "Of course, my darling. Where else would you go?"

He stared at her challengingly. "All right. I'm back. But on my own terms. I'm moving into the spare bedroom. We will share a life and a house together—but not a bed, not ever again. Is that understood?"

She cocked her head, regarding him like an inquisitive bird. "If that's how you want it, dear."

He was still challenging her. "If I want to fuck somebody, I fuck somebody. Just like you've been doing for years."

Her head remained cocked in sweet regard. "So that's where you've been. Screwing some hot-cunted little chippy

164

you've had your eye on, but never had the nerve until now to do anything about."

"No," he said angrily. Remembering his resolution that he would not let her make him angry, he became angrier still. "I only wish I had."

"Go right ahead, darling." Her voice remained coolly amused. "Just keep your nose clean, if you can't keep your cock in your pants. Don't believe for a minute I'll save you from Daddy's righteous wrath if you get caught out."

Still angry, he got to his feet. "I'm tired. I'm going to bed."

He went into their bedroom to move his things. He tramped back and forth sullenly, seeing in passage that she rose only to fix a drink for herself. What he had hoped would be a victory of sorts had become, because of her sardonic confidence in his return, a defeat instead. But, in sullen acceptance, he knew also that he would find a way to live through his life as Eleanor had shaped it, too long ago for a profound change now.

And, he comforted himself, I will have *her* one more time.

When he had finished, he took a long shower, put on a bathrobe, and went into the kitchen to make a nightcap. A strong nightcap, for he needed desperately to sleep.

"What about dinner, dear?" Eleanor asked, still sitting on the couch. "I can stir us up something quick, if you'd like."

"I don't want dinner," he said, though at the suggestion he was instantly aware of hunger. He couldn't remember the last time he had eaten.

As he drank the last ice-rattling dregs of the nightcap, and reached over to turn out the light, Eleanor brought a hamburger and a glass of milk on a tray. He did not protest because the smell of the food had made him ravenously hungry.

She watched while he sat on the side of the bed, the sheet pulled up to hide his nakedness, and ate the hamburger.

Moving to the door, she paused. "Comfy?" she inquired with a provocative smile. When he glared at her without

165

answering, she disappeared. He turned out the light, assuring himself in the darkness that he knew what Eleanor was up to. She meant to have him safely back in a shared bed before the boys came home from football camp. She won't win that one, he told himself as he drowsed into well-fed sleep.

He didn't know how late it was when he became aware of her mouth. Still half-submerged in sleep, he experienced it first as a dream of *her* mouth pulsating so sweetly on his engorged flesh. Only when the hot response of his throbbing cock became too vivid for continued slumber did his confused mind realize that it was Eleanor, it *must* be Eleanor; *she* could not possibly be with him, for *she* had insisted on being with her husband.

He struggled, then, against Eleanor's seductive mouth, having to fight himself as much as he was fighting her because he had fully wakened much too late. Eleanor slyly put a warm hand under his balls, stroking in the tenderest spot of all. Against his will, he began to come. Her throat pulsed greedily, drinking him as she always drank down his come.

He groaned, fading into flaccid surrender. Eleanor's mouth remained on him, savoring his maleness though it was soft now, finished. Finally, still in darkness, she rose up, sated as a vampire, from his flesh. Her voice whispered, "No other woman will ever do you as good, my dear. That's why you'll never leave me."

She went away, and again he was half-asleep. In the depths of drowsiness he answered her silently in triumph: "But there is, Eleanor. *Her*. And there will be others, Eleanor. There will always be others."

The Woman:

It was the last emotion she could have expected. But, entering her house, she knew that what she was feeling was a deep, true happiness of the soul.

Impossible, but real. She should have carried in her heart, at the least, the sadness of parting. Today had been truly a parting despite the fact that she had promised *him* —promised herself—one last beautiful Thursday.

She stood in her kitchen, searching vainly the familiar environment of home for the source of the happiness. Hale would be here in a couple of hours; next week, the Gold Dust Twins would be coming home, brown and rambunctious, from summer camp. Soon now, too soon, it would be time to buy school clothes.

Then she looked inside herself, and found it. *She was free.*

She didn't know exactly how, or why, it had happened. Even *when*. She simply looked inside herself, to find there a freedom she had never known—for it was a freedom of the soul.

No guilts, no fears, no hidden places where she was not good enough. I can take a man or I can *not* take a man, after *he* is gone, she told herself in glee. I can love, I can be loved. I can even love Hale, as I have never loved Hale. *For I am free.*

Humming, she set about cooking dinner. When she fed him, she was gratified by Hale's pleasure in the eating. She watched Hale settle down to his nightly load of work before retreating happily into her bedroom. Choosing her filmiest nightgown, she got into bed prepared to let her mind wander enchantingly over Next Thursday, when they would come together for the last and most wonderful time of all.

Which, she realized, was a large piece of the happiness. She had accepted the Ending as she had accepted the

Beginning. The only part left to do was for them to make it as good as it ought to be, that Beginning and Ending would be all of a piece.

It did not disturb her when she saw Hale coming out of the bathroom with his bottom bare.

"I'm sorry," she said regretfully. "But I can't, tonight."

"Oh," he said with the rueful understanding of a husband. "I didn't know . . ."

She laughed because he looked so woebegone. "Come here," she said tenderly. "I'll take care of your problem."

Hale got into bed. She came to him, busily unbuttoning his pajama top. "I want you naked all over," she said firmly. "I am getting so damned tired of sleeping with a man who, at the best of times, is always half dressed."

Hale allowed her to take off the pajama top. Stirred by the unexpected warmth of her invitation, he already had a hard-on. In the lamplight, she looked at his plump, hairless chest. The male buds were as pinkly erect now, she saw in surprise, as hers became when she was aroused. On a sudden impulse, she put her mouth on his nipple. He gasped, squirming away, then surrendered to the sensation.

His flesh tasted salty. She flicked her tongue against his nipple, caught it lightly between her teeth, felt him shudder violently. Her hand slipped down his rounded stomach to grasp his cock, triumphantly feeling his body tremble again.

Oh, wonderful, he loves it, she thought in glee. He doesn't know yet, either, what's coming next. She wanted to laugh, but she could not laugh, for her mouth was too busy with the hard little nipple.

She drew away at last, sliding smoothly down to poise in anticipation over his cock. She gazed upon it with avid curiosity, for in all their years she had never actually viewed it in detail. Hale had been circumcised, showing the blood-pink head turgid with desire. Smaller, both in length and in girth, than *his* beautiful cock. But a man's cock, nevertheless.

She gave him a mischievous glance from her poised

position. She read with glee the stunned look in his eyes, heard the unbelieving gasp of his breath as she suddenly swallowed him whole. His body arched against her face and, though hanging on, she had to ease off to keep from choking. Oh yes! It was a cock, all right.

She took her mouth away to grin at him. "Didn't think I knew how to do that, did you?"

Before he could answer, she was on him again; gently this time, sliding her pursed lips up and down. His hands gripped her head, pressing her mouth deeply into his groin. She felt his deep sigh as he began to come; with an incredible sensation of fulfillment she tasted his come in her mouth.

"My God!" he said softly. "Where did you learn to do that?"

She smiled sweetly through bruised and tender lips. "I've *always* known. You just never asked for it, that's all."

He regarded her with awed wonder. "But, if you knew about it, why didn't you just . . . ?"

She moved up beside him to put her arms around his plump body. "Go to sleep," she urged gently. "You'll sleep well now."

She held him until she heard his gentle snore. Only then did she roll carefully away to her side of the bed, as satisfied in the flesh as if she had been fucked a dozen times by a dozen men.

And that's something else I've learned, she thought deeply. To give is to get. The more you give, the more you get. And . . . I have so much lust, so much love, to give.

The Two:

He had suggested they meet at the cabin. She had not wanted it that way.

"Let's meet today, here at the end, where we met in the beginning," she had told him over the telephone. "I want you to ride your bike, too."

He had chuckled. "You're not planning to run me down again?"

"No," she had answered soberly. "Of course not."

She had been happy, however, to know that, just because he was seeing her today, he could laugh. Even if it had to be for the last time.

She arrived fifteen minutes early. Not because she could not wait, but because she needed the time, on this particularly dear spot of earth, to think about *him;* about herself; about the Two.

She was still happy. She was still free. Yet there was in this day a sadness of ending, palpable in her heart as in her soul. Yet the sadness did not change in the least the fact of Ending.

Her heart gave a leap when, far in the distance, she saw him coming on the bicycle. He was wearing the pale blue shorts, too tight and too short for a man his age. His hairy, muscular legs pumping steadily, his head down, he was driving at her straight on, as his cock drove straight on into her hot pussy. He was a bullet of passion, speeding to meet her.

Only at the moment of arrival did he lift his head to see her waiting behind the wheel of the station wagon. He was sweating from the exertion. It was good to sweat on this hot day. In the cabin, their bodies would stick together, in his nostrils would be her hot female odor.

He gripped the brakes, sliding the bicycle to a skidding halt beside the open window of the car. He gazed, smiling, into her face.

"Hello. Waiting for somebody?"

"Yes," she said, with that intense look in her eyes that meant she was hot to fuck. "Waiting for you."

She gave him the ring of car keys so he could put the bicycle into the rear of the station wagon. She waited until he slid in beside her. With him came the scent of male sweat; it raised the hackles on her nape, she felt between her legs the warm ooze of desire.

They did not kiss. She took the keys, started the engine, and began driving toward today's place for making love: the cabin where they had first fucked, so unsatisfactorily in the beginning, so wonderfully in the end.

He had brought words ready to be spoken, the message he had worked toward realizing all this long week. Sitting beside her, sensing her intense desire—indeed, feeling himself so acutely attuned to her being that he thought he could *smell* her heat—he found it extraordinarily difficult to speak.

"There's . . . something I know. Now. You must have realized it, too, by this time," he said hesitantly.

She turned her head briefly, but did not answer.

He stirred uncomfortably. "It's . . . Eleanor won't be enough for me, not ever again. No more than your husband will be enough for you."

"Yes," she said. "But it doesn't change anything."

He leaned toward her in urgency. "It means we can go on together. That we *must* go on."

She sat still, automatically steering the car for so long that he could not hold his breath long enough. Even then she did not speak; she simply placed one hand tight up into his crotch to stroke the clothed outline of his cock.

"Give it to me," she said.

He stretched his legs to move the zipper and bring his cock into the open. Her warm, damp palm gripped his naked flesh.

Her eyes were straight ahead on the road. "It's beyond talking about. Don't you understand that?"

"But . . . *why?*" he said desperately.

Her hand moved on him, her damp palm fucking him in

the movement. "Because today we are going to have the best of each other, body and soul," she said quietly. "Going on would mean hanging on to something that wouldn't be quite the best. That's not good enough. Not for me and you."

Her hand was again holding him, not gripping hard, simply caressing his hardness.

"You know what will happen," he said. "I'll go looking for you in other women. You'll look for me in other men. Because what we've had together, both of us know, won't be found at home."

"Yes. We probably will. And maybe, once in a while, we'll discover in some stranger a small piece of what we have shared." Her voice, so calm and thoughtful, left him nothing more to say.

When they arrived, he moved to get out. She sat still; she had words for *him* now, a message in reply to his futile message. It, too, might be futile. But she had to try. Beyond these last spoken words would be only the language of the flesh.

"The ending with each other has nothing to do with my husband or your wife," she told him slowly, carefully, for only slowly and carefully had she herself come to understand it. "It is only mine, it is only yours. For the last time today you will fit into my fantasy of lust, for the last time I will fit into yours. For this one last time, we can be as *unreal* to each other as we are *real*. Both the real and the unreal are so important that, without them, you-and-I can no longer exist."

"I don't understand that."

"I don't understand it, either," she answered serenely. "But that's how it is."

She took his hand. "Come on, now. Let's fuck."

They walked hand in hand up the steps into the cabin, going directly into the bedroom. Separating herself, she began slowly, before his eyes, to take off her clothes.

He stood watching her body as it was revealed to him. Her breasts were perfect, the pink nipples standing up boldly in their tiny lust to be sucked and nibbled at. She had the most beautiful belly he had ever seen, slightly rounded, sloping sweetly into her hip joints, into the shading of pubic hair. Her legs, so long and slender, would soon lift around him, clenching him in the scissor-lock of her need to be fucked deeply, deeply, and forever.

He could see the tiny quiverings of her thigh muscles as she stood naked, giving herself to his gaze as, soon, she would give herself to his cock.

"Now you," she whispered. "Let me see *you*."

He bent swiftly to pull the T-shirt over his head. Her breath caught at the sight of the hairy chest, the rippling muscles of his biceps. Fine curls of hair, as though luminescent, glowed golden on his forearms. His rib cage was lean with ribbed musculature, the pelt of hair on his chest arrowing down his belly to the loins.

He unzipped the shorts, let them drop. His cock sprang up to thump against his belly, hard and throbbing. She bit her lower lip, gazing raptly at that great male tool, feeling it already probing, a hot branding-iron, into her pussy.

He came to her, kneeling, putting both arms around her loins to clasp her belly to his face. She felt his deep chest movements as he breathed in her odor of female flesh. Putting both hands on his tousled head, she pressed it against her belly.

"Take me to the bed," she whispered.

He rose, lifting her. She felt light and free with the marvelous strength of his lifting. Her breath locked in her body in anticipation as he moved three steps, carrying her light-as-air weight, to lay her down gently on the bare mattress.

She would not let go when he laid her down, clinging with all the lustful strength of her need, making him lie down in her. She did not want his kiss, his touch; she had no need of foreplay to prepare her for the advent of his cock. So she told him, in plain and simple words, not to kiss her, not to touch her, simply to fuck her, *fuck her*, and keep on fucking her until all fucking was ended.

She opened her legs and closed them around his lean hips, taking his cock all the way in with the first thrust,

173

feeling it slide into her, hot and alive. The walls of her pussy were already in trembling retreat from the thrust, yet grabbing like a small hand when she sensed his cock slipping away, only to know that it was returning in a thrust stronger, deeper, than the first thrust.

So they fucked, in silence and in love, each swing of his hips a full and complete stroke. Her loins began bucking and yielding under him as their bodies melded together in the hot lust for fucking that dwelled equally within their minds.

So it began and so it went on, sweetly, lustfully, and for a time they remained unconscious of the quickening pace. They were oblivious to the rhythmic jangle of the old bedsprings, the roughness of the mattress under her back. Indeed, they fucked unaware of the world about them, for there was only the fucking forever. Their breathing mingled into one breath, as their bodies were merged into one body, so that he was no longer the Man, she was no longer the Woman, they were simply the One that was the Two.

But no human fucking can be forever; the pace began building; he was driving more strongly, with a harder cock. With each stroke, his response to the pulsations of her pussy was so sensuous he could bear it no longer. Bear it he did, however; until, somewhere halfway across forever, he sensed that, far back in her deepest being, she was beginning to come. He was glad, for he had to come, too, he *must* come now, or he would die.

He began to ride with her, taking her rhythm, so that she was fucking him more than he was fucking her, digging her heels into the small of his back to take his throbbing cock deeper into her turbulent vitals.

Recognizing instinctively that he was waiting for her, she quickened, wanting more than his cock—any man's cock —could give her; she wanted the greatest fucking of all time. Reaching for it, dreaming it true as she was living it true, *he* was no longer *him* but simply *Cock*, for she was indeed achieving the greatest fucking of all time.

Because she was getting it, she began giving it back tenfold. With a skip of her gasping heart, she felt him leap

174

over the threshold of no return, taking away from her the rhythm and the drive, dominating her female flesh as it yearned, in this moment, to be dominated. The great flailing cock, whipping in and whipping out, began coming in great bursts of scalding hot come—at least it felt scalding hot, so that her senses whirled, she could only hang on as she entered helplessly into an orgasm to match his magnificent ejaculation.

The Two did not know how long it went on before they crumpled together, finished, their bodies wedded by the sweating skin of their flesh, and she was weeping softly for the great accomplishment and the great loss that was theirs in this day of ending.

While she wept, clinging to him, he began slowly to fuck her with the half-soft erection, feeling her dripping wet with their mingled come as his cock moved in her, so tender and alive he wanted to scream with the goodness of it. Without warning, in the midst of weeping, she clutched at, achieved, a greedy little Number Two orgasm that surprised her with its vehement unexpectedness.

It made them laugh. In the relief of shared laughter, he murmured, "Greedy little bitch," as they lay together, his half-limp cock simply nice in her now, not utterly needed. They were drowsily content, the peace of completion in their souls as in their flesh, and without knowing they were going to do it, in two minutes they were asleep, *with* each other as truly in the sleeping as they had been with each other in the fucking.

She came awake to the sensation of his mouth on her clitoris. It was the way she had desired to wake up, for she had been dreaming of his mouth on her, sucking sweetly. She writhed and opened under him as his tongue, in reality as in dream, flickered deeply.

It made her hungry to taste his cock. She pulled herself up and over, as he turned under her to continue lapping at her quivering cunt, to take his cock into her mouth in one smooth gulp. It was not hard, but her sliding lips soon took care of that small problem. His face buried in her muff, she spread herself open to him and her mouth began fucking

175

his cock in rhythm with the movement of his tongue on her clitoris.

It went on and on, replete with the ecstasy of sensation but not urgent, so that it seemed possible to continue forever. But at last, his arms gripping her thighs to turn her under, he switched ends so that they were face to face, and for the first time today she tasted his lips, kissing him as greedily as she had sucked at his beautiful great cock.

He was in her again now, not quite knowing how he—or maybe she—had effected the penetration. He smiled when she asked, giggling, "Did we invent sixty-nine?" and answered, "Yes. We just invented sixty-nine. Think we could get a patent on the process?" She murmured, "Mmm, yes, let's do that, I *like* sixty-nine. Except I couldn't decide which end to concentrate on."

Free and easy this time in the fucking, no need to go anywhere because they were already there. He let her have a good orgasm all by herself because he wasn't sure he could get another one; the first, so complete, had taken everything he had, perhaps a little more.

After a while, he decided maybe it was possible, after all, and, some little time after that, he thought he'd die if he *didn't* get it, desperately he was begging, "Help me, goddamn it, help me, help me . . ." She was laughing, fucking hard under him; one hand reached down to stroke his balls, and that was all the help he needed; he exploded in her with a sudden violence.

He had now achieved a strange state of being which he had never reached with any woman. With absolutely no need for another orgasm, his cock remained reasonably erect and willing. He could, for the first time in his life fuck a woman—*this* woman, *her*—without the self-generated pressure to prove his maleness by ejaculation that, like most men, had been always present during the act of love.

With such an intense sensibility of the flesh and of the mind, he could savor the subtleties of her textures and temperatures. There was a tiny rough place, very deep, that pulsated every time he pressed it—and a softness, just at the entrance, that soothed her, slowed her down to wait for the next deep reach of his cock's head. It was wonderful to explore her so subtly, yet so completely.

She sensed the change in him from the hard driving of before to the exploration of now. It allowed her also an equal degree of exploration, shifting under him, taking him deep, taking him shallow, reveling in the long smooth tube of male flesh her body had swallowed up.

So they fucked forever, gently, sweetly, tenderly, with no nagging sense of the inexorable passage of their time, until at last, gently and sweetly and tenderly, the fucking was finished.

Both the Man and the Woman—the Two—knew it in the same instant of completion. Without regret, they withdrew from each other's flesh. She rolled over immediately to study the westerly slant of sunlight through an undraped window.

"Oh my God! It's terribly late," she gasped. "We'll have to hurry."

They hurried, yet without a great hurry in their souls. They took showers, in cold water because the water heater was not on, they got into their clothes and then into the station wagon, and the cabin was forever behind them, as the fucking had now also become a part of their past.

She stopped the station wagon in exactly the same spot she had stopped the first time. They sat side by side in this moment of parting, until he said, "Can't we . . . ?"

She put her hand to his mouth. "Don't say it," she whispered with trembling lips. She strengthened her voice. "It can't possibly go on beyond a fucking like the fucking we've had today." She shook her head fatefully. "There is a time for Ending, as there is a time for Beginning. We've had both. So go on now. *Go on.*"

She wanted to cry, he knew. But she was not crying. Quietly he said, "All right, then," opened the car door and stepped out.

She watched, without getting from behind the wheel, as he retrieved the bicycle, paused to return the keys.

"Go on now." Her voice trembled with the words. "Go on, damn it."

"I love you," he said, simply and forever. Angling the heft of his body onto the pedal, he mounted as he began to depart from her. He did not look back, not even once, for now he was gone forever.

"I love you, too," she said aloud after his departing figure. She waited until he was out of sight. Then she started the engine and drove home.

So it ended as it had begun, as all things mortal must end; becoming not-to-be in love and sorrow and lust. Not with regret; in this small breath of time encompassed by one moon of her flesh, the Two had been alive in the desire of their blood to mate in their flesh and, for that briefly sweet time, the world was a beautiful place, perceived as beautiful by heightened senses.

It was not, and then it was; then it was-no-more. Each person of the Two, absent from the felicity of the other, surely would seek the perfection of love and lust they had known together; because now they both know it can, it does, exist.

But . . . will either find it again in another brief, imperfect human body? Not even their deepest, their truest, hearts can know the answer.

HER

Anonymous

Rarely in the history of book publishing has a love story been told with the frankness and earthy honesty of *Her*, the adult love story that explores the lust, the passion, the ecstasy and the longing between a woman and a man – a book that portrays the beauty, the joy and the truth to be found in sensual love.

HIM

Anonymous

After *Her* there could only be *Him* . . .

Every man and every woman contain two beings: the animal and the human; the spiritual and the bestial. Only when the two come together can a man or a woman experience true, sensual, ecstatic love.

Him is the story of two women and one man, who together shared a love affair that awakened them to a new world of carnality and lust – and that freed the primitive, sensual self of each.